Th___ ___AGE DONE

THE DAMAGE DONE

LINDA NEWBERY

SCHOLASTIC
PRESS

Scholastic Children's Books,
Commonwealth House, 1–19 New Oxford Street,
London WC1A 1NU, UK
a division of Scholastic Ltd
London - New York - Toronto - Sydney - Auckland
Mexico City - New Delhi - Hong Kong

First published in the UK by Scholastic Ltd, 2001

Quotation from Equus © Peter Shaffer, 1973

ISBN 0 439 99799 2

Typeset by M Rules
Printed by Cox and Wyman Ltd, Reading, Berks.

10 9 8 7 6 5 4 3 2 1

For Kathleen Peyton,
who made me want to try

"The only thing I know is this:
a horse's head is finally unknowable to me.
Yet I handle children's heads – which I must
presume to be more complicated. . ."

Peter Shaffer, *Equus*

CHAPTER 1

One night before Easter, when the air smelled of earth and spring rain, the fear came back.

She thought she had beaten them, her night fears. They belonged to the long nights of winter, to the dark, timeless hours when her own bedroom turned against her and became hostile. Now, again, she was hurled into wakefulness by a harsh, single image that thrust itself into her brain. A cry snagged in her throat as she lurched upright, her pulse thumping against her ears.

A dream.

The silence of the night sidled up to her, prickled her skin. She sat on the edge of her bed and concentrated on breathing. A flick of the light switch threw the room into bright, unnatural normality. Her watch said it was half-past one. Four, four-and-a-half hours of darkness to come; she wouldn't sleep now.

Kirsty fumbled her feet into her slippers and stood up.

Along the landing, she saw the crack of light under the door of her father's study. Faintly, she smelled cigarette smoke. He said he didn't smoke any more, but she knew he did, late at night when he was working. She didn't need to catch him doing it. The dead-ash smell hung in the air, in the curtains, even though he opened the windows wide every morning. She could hear the faint clacking of his keyboard; that meant he was working, not just staring into space.

She couldn't disturb him. For most of the day he prowled about, restless and irritable, waiting for these few productive hours.

She went to the loo, washed her face and briefly looked at herself in the mirror. Only briefly. It was when she studied her reflection more intently, looked into her own eyes, that the fears started taking hold – stupid fears, that seemed ridiculous in daylight.

The house seemed so empty now. The floorboards creaked as she went back to her own room, past the open door of Jay's room. Her feet were cold. Getting quickly back into bed, she clicked a cassette into her Walkman, pulled the duvet up around her shoulders, and wished she had something to read. In winter, she'd always kept a pile of books on her bedside table – mostly the sex-and-shopping blockbusters favoured by her friend Lottie. Nothing at all demanding, certainly nothing disturbing. She'd given them back now. Dad had shelves piled with books, but they were in his study, and she couldn't go in there while he was working.

There was no one she could talk to.

That day she met Dally.

CHAPTER 2

Out in the April-fresh morning, the anxiety of the wakeful night slipped out of Kirsty's thoughts. She walked back to the house from the stables, seeing the lawn dew-wet and glistening; she saw a blackbird's darting run across the grass, and the trees' first haze of leaf. She walked slowly, deeply content. This was her reward for having endured the winter, for the months of getting up while it was still dark, breaking the ice on the water-troughs, shivering her feet into wellingtons to go out and check the horses last thing at night. She thought of breakfast, then Mrs Hendy's and the shopping, the feed order and the bills. Her day, safe and ordinary.

The kitchen door was open, and both cats were sunning themselves on the mat, waiting for their breakfast. The house, Bramblings, was now divided into two, and the originally large garden had been halved by a fence and high trellis. The Richmonds, who lived on the other side, had designer gravel and architectural plants and a pagoda; Kirsty's and her father's half was much as it had always been, grass and shrubs, with a swathe of daffodils just past flowering and in need of dead-heading. Kirsty preferred it this way, just as she preferred their own half of the house, shabby and cluttered, to the rather austere elegance beyond the dividing wall. The Richmonds, who both worked in London and were often away throughout the week, were just playing at living in the country, according to Kirsty's friend Lottie. They both had brand-new green wellies for their Sunday walks, and Julian had a Barbour hat that made him look like a hunt supporter. They sometimes came down to look at the horses, but complained when the wind blew the smell from the dung heap into their garden. Kirsty had offered them free manure to make up for it, forgetting that they only grew Mediterranean plants that preferred dry gravel. Fiona had thought they might try riding lessons, and had been surprised when Kirsty told them that there were no horses for them to ride. Of the seven horses and ponies kept here, six belonged to other people; the seventh, owned by Kirsty's brother Jay, was a neurotic thoroughbred recovering from a tendon injury.

"You'll get disgustingly *horsey*," Kirsty's other friend, Tatjana, had complained when Kirsty decided not to stay on into the sixth form. "You won't have anything to talk about except Badminton and the price of hay."

But Kirsty didn't think of herself as particularly horsey. She had no horse of her own; she only rode out when one of the liveries needed exercising, and then it was quietly by herself or sometimes with Lottie. Jay was the horsey one in the family, or what was left of the family: he was the one who had started it all. At first a few liveries; now he had ambitions to turn Bramblings into an upmarket livery yard and training centre. But he had taken himself off to Connecticut, and meanwhile, Kirsty was running the stables. Running the house, too, because it suited her father, and because it suited her – not having to make the effort to do anything else.

She kicked off her boots outside the back door and went inside, tripping over cats. She forked out cat food from a tin, then put coffee in the filter and filled the machine with water. She made the coffee strong, the way her father liked it, enough to last him till mid-morning. She wrote *coffee* on the shopping list and looked in the money jar. Only five pound coins; not enough for everything on her list.

The phone rang while she was eating her toast. She waited a few seconds to see if her father was going to answer it upstairs; then, when he didn't, she picked up. Her mother's voice said briskly, "Darling, I thought I'd catch you. Isn't Graham there?"

"Haven't seen him this morning, yet," Kirsty said. "Do you want him?"

"No, it's you I want to talk to. I thought we might see each other over Easter. How about coming to stay, just for a couple of nights? Phil and I think you could do with a break. Graham can look after things there, can't he?"

Kirsty saw London streets thick with taxis and buses and crowds; she pictured herself trapped in a tube train, with the doors closing. Panic tightened her throat.

"What's it got to do with Phil?" she said. "Anyway, I can't. There's too much to do here." Her mother had no *idea*, if she thought it possible to abandon the place for a couple of days. As for her father looking after the horses – he was far too clueless and impractical. "Anyway," she added, "there's a mare due to foal any day now –"

"But darling, I hardly *see* you, these days. Is it really essential for you to be there full-time?"

"Yes! Something might go wrong. And besides, there's a pony on full livery now – the owner's really fussy. I've got to be here!"

"Well, in that case," Kirsty's mother said crisply, "Phil and I will have to come over. We'll take you out to lunch. You don't object to that, I hope?"

Kirsty looked around at the comforting clutter of the kitchen: the cork noticeboard with multi-layered leaflets and postcards, a jug of primroses on the window-sill, the tailless cloth mouse on the floor by the cat basket. She imagined her mother's and Phil's kitchen as hi-tech, with gleaming surfaces and cooking utensils hanging in place as precisely as surgeon's implements. "I'll think about it and ring you back, shall I?" she stalled.

"No, let's sort it out now. Saturday?"

"It's always busy here at weekends—"

"Saturday," her mother said firmly. "We'll see you about half-past twelve. Graham can stand in for an hour or two – that's hardly too much to expect of him. Is he working?"

"What, now, you mean? I shouldn't think so, it's early for him."

"I don't mean *now*. I mean is he actually doing any work?"

"Oh yes. He works every night. At least, he's in his study every night."

Kirsty heard her mother's scornful exhalation. "That's hardly the same thing. Surfing the web, more likely."

"No, he does work," Kirsty said, though she had little idea. She waited for her mother to say, in her barbed tone, "And is he *drinking*?" but the question remained unasked.

"Anyway, Mum, I've got to go." With the phone wedged between neck and shoulder, Kirsty poured her father's coffee. Black, with sugar. "Look, I'll phone you back later about coming down, shall I?"

Her mother wouldn't be put off. "See you on Saturday. Half-past twelve. And wear something decent." Her tone softened. "Bye then, darling. I'll look forward to it. We both will."

One of the cats, Moth, was twining himself around Kirsty's legs. She replaced the phone and picked him up, holding his plump warm body close, so that the throb of his purring seemed part of herself. Saturday. Out for lunch. She thought of the village pub, close and unthreatening, and then of the sort of place her mother would prefer – smart, expensive, probably involving a car journey. She saw herself a prisoner in the back of Phil's Jaguar.

The cat struggled to be put down. Kirsty took her father's coffee upstairs, finding him in the study. He was still in his dressing-gown, tousle-haired and unshaven: not working, but surfing the net, just as Ursula had said.

"Hi, love. Was that the phone just now?"

"Yes, it was Mum." Kirsty put the coffee mug next to his mouse mat, noticing a manilla folder with scribbled notes spilling out. *THE DAMAGE DONE*, he had written on the folder, in his bold black writing with great swooping capital Ds. "How's it going?" she asked casually.

He looked at the folder. "OK. Yes, OK, I think. There's one or two things you might help me with later. What did Ursula want?"

"She wanted me to go and stay with her for Easter, at the flat. Of course, I said no. But she's coming on Saturday to take me out for lunch. With Phil."

"Oh, God." Her father yawned and pushed a hand back through his hair, making a tuft of it stand up. "We'd better have a bit of a tidy-up, then."

We, Kirsty thought. That meant her. Her father never did any tidying-up, apart from pushing his books and papers into a heap.

"I don't suppose she'll come in. I need some money, for shopping," she told him. "But I've got to go to Mrs Hendy's first."

"My wallet. There's a tenner in there. That be enough?"

"Thanks." Kirsty found the jacket slung on a chair in her father's bedroom, and took out the note. Then he called her back into the study.

8

"Oh – Saturday, did you say? I'll be out, most of the day."

Kirsty knew what that meant. "At Clare's?"

Graham nodded. "Adam's home from university. It's his birthday – she's cooking a special lunch. You could probably come if you wanted. You haven't met him, have you? Clare wouldn't mind." He looked at her from under his eyebrows. "He's quite a hunk, apparently. Clare says so. You might like to check for yourself."

"Clare's his mum. She's biased."

"D'you want me to ask if you can come?"

Kirsty shook her head. All this *eating*, she thought; all this lunch. Why do people make such a fuss about it? It's only food. A bowl of soup and a piece of cheese in the kitchen would do just as well. Briefly, she wondered whether she could use Clare's special lunch as a reason to put off her mother; but no, better to get it over with. One outing now might stop Mum from pestering her to go to London. "I'm off, then," she told Graham. "See you later."

She pushed the ten-pound note into her jeans pocket with the coins and went downstairs for the shopping list. She used the village shop for odd items like bread during the week, cycling there and carrying the stuff back in her rucksack; her father did the main shopping at the big Sainsbury's on the edge of Newington, eight miles away. Today, she was going to Ravenswood first, then the shop.

Ravenswood, on the other edge of the village, was an imposing stone house, set well back from the lane and approached by a gravel drive between yew hedges. It was early eighteenth-century, her father said, and must once have needed a whole squad of servants to run it. Now, it was the home of one elderly woman, Mrs Hendy. She was looked after by a daily housekeeper/companion, Mrs Bishop who could only have been a few years younger. She, too, lived alone, in a cottage next to the Old Forge antiques shop.

That's what I am, Kirsty thought, cycling past the cottage. A housekeeper/companion, for Dad. Mrs Bishop had been at Ravenswood for years, greying and fading. Eventually Mrs Hendy, who must be in her eighties, would die, and then Mrs Bishop would have nothing to do. What about me? Kirsty thought. What's going to happen to me?

Her tyres crunched on gravel as she reached Ravenswood's driveway. Rounding the curve of the yew tunnel, she looked at the austere stone frontage of the house, its entrance portico flanked by rows of windows. It was an enormous house for one person. Before he left, Jay had brought her round to meet Mrs Hendy, who looked forbidding – frail, stooped with age, but with a beaky nose and imperious, darting eyes. She had invited them in for sherry, into a sitting-room that looked to Kirsty as comfortless as a stately home, with huge framed portraits and three identical sofas, velvet, with scrolled armrests, placed squarely round a fireplace. Jay, when he'd been the one to look after the horse, had regularly gone in for a glass of sherry, every Friday – he had told Kirsty that Mrs Hendy, who didn't see many people, had looked forward to it, a social occasion. But Jay was seven years older than Kirsty, and Mrs Hendy thought Kirsty was a child. She had said so, quite bluntly: "You don't look old enough to have left school!" and had looked her up and down with haughty eyes. Jay had pointed out that Kirsty was seventeen, and perfectly capable of taking care of one old horse.

Now Kirsty had the keys to the feed-room and harness-room, and there was no reason to see Mrs Hendy. She went up to the house only at the end of each week, to collect her money from Mrs Bishop in the kitchen.

She turned down the smaller gravelled track that led round the side of the house to the stables and outbuildings. The gardens at the rear were magnificent, sloping down to a lake. There was an immense sweep of lawn, with a specimen cedar spreading inky branches. The borders nearer the house were bright with spring bulbs; on the opposite side from the stables there was a separate walled garden, through whose entrance Kirsty glimpsed a length of straight border and a topiary peacock. Beyond the lake was meadowland, grazed by cattle, with an alder-fringed stream running through. Who looked after it all, she wondered? It was the sort of house that once would have had teams of gardeners, growing roses for the vases indoors, and hot-house peaches. It was rather sad, Kirsty thought:

all this splendour just for one old lady, who, from her appearance – neat skirt, court shoes, pearl necklace – rarely went outside. The garden was opened to the public once a year, but otherwise it was kept hidden and private. I could come here, Kirsty thought, at dawn, and walk across the lawn and stand by the lake. No one would know, unless Mrs Hendy gets up very early. I could swim here, by myself, when it first gets light. She imagined herself taking off her clothes in the trailing canopy of the willows, and slipping into the cool water. Like Ophelia, in the painting Tatjana had on her bedroom wall. But Ophelia had kept her clothes on, and had drowned herself. Tat was doing *Hamlet* for English AS-Level; she and Kirsty had watched the video, the one with Helena Bonham-Carter as poor mad Ophelia.

There was only one horse at Ravenswood, an old chestnut hunter called Prince, who belonged to Mrs Hendy's son and was now retired. Like Mrs Hendy, he lived in splendid isolation, in a stableyard that must have once housed a whole family's horses and a carriage besides. All the stable doors except one were closed and padlocked – a terrible waste, Jay had said, with ideas of leasing them for an extension of his livery business. Prince, staring slacklipped at the pigeons that pecked on the gravel, brightened when he saw Kirsty and pawed at the floor of his stable. He must be bored, she thought, without horse company; he would be happier if she took him home to

Bramblings, where he could rough it with the others. Instead, he spent each day out by himself in the post-and-railed paddock, grazing and dozing, thinking whatever a horse thought.

Kirsty fetched his feed of cubes and crushed barley from the feed-room and mucked out his stable while he ate. It was a beautiful old-fashioned stable, with herringbone flooring in red brick and a fixed hay-rack. Everything was in marked contrast to the stables at home, which had been converted from a cowshed and pig-sties, most with wonky doors, uneven floors and stubborn bolts. Judging that it was warm enough for Prince to do without his rug, she led him out to the field. She left the straw bedding piled up at the back of his stable, for the floor to dry, but filled the hay-rack ready for the evening.

She had used up the last of a bale. The hay was stored in an open-sided barn at the far end of the outbuildings; she hauled out two more bales to take to the feed-room, then fetched a wheelbarrow. While she was hoisting the second bale on top of the first, balancing the barrow, she heard a clumping sound behind her in the yard.

She turned. Someone came out of the harness-room. She saw dark clothing, a skinny body; then the figure turned in her direction. She had a quick impression of a bony face, intense eyes, a tangle of brown hair. He looked at her for a moment, then walked away quickly, along the drive to the house.

Kirsty stared after him. An intruder?

She shouldn't be here. She fought the urge to get on her bike and hurtle back to Bramblings. Jay shouldn't have made her come here. Her hands were trembling, her throat tight and dry. But who would look after Prince if she ran away and refused to come back?

She gripped the handles of the barrow to steady herself, and trundled up to the feed-store. Leaving the hay, she stepped cautiously into the harness-room, which had been locked until she arrived half an hour ago. Nothing stolen – Prince's saddle and bridle, cleaned and unused, hung on their pegs; his rugs were folded on a trunk, the grooming kit in its box. Then she realized.

The boy, or man, had clumped down the ladder from the loft above. He must have been there all the time, while she had been mucking out the stable. He might have been watching her.

Her skin prickled. Her fear was at odds with the familiar warm smell of horse-sweat and leather.

Carefully she climbed the steps of the ladder, and lifted the hatch into the loft. She heard the stirring of mice, smelled musty hay and dust; the loft had once been the hay-store, reached by high wooden doors through which bales could be pitched in straight from the cart. Now, it was just another storage place. Her eyes adjusting to the gloom, Kirsty made out another trunk, boxes, blankets, coils of twine.

She would have to tell Mrs Hendy.

Clumping down again, she slid the bolt across to secure the hatchway. Then, for speed, and in case the intruder were still lurking somewhere, she took her bike, and rode to the back door of the house.

There was an ancient enamel bell-push here. Kirsty pressed it, and heard a bell jingling deep inside the house with a sound that emphasized silence and emptiness. Then she saw that the door was ajar. She slipped inside, into a kind of vestibule with coat-hooks and umbrella stands and rows of boots and shoes. Next, a scullery, with a huge sink, a washing-machine and a tumble-drier. Another door led, she supposed, to the kitchen. She hesitated; the door opened, and Mrs Bishop stood there, in a pink overall pulled tight across her chest.

"Hello," Kirsty said. "I've just been dong Prince's stable and I saw someone down there, in the yard. I thought I'd better tell Mrs Hendy."

Mrs Bishop had a vague, kindly face. "What sort of some-one?" she asked, without much interest.

"A bloke, tall, skinny. Youngish. In jeans, and a black jacket that looked too small."

"Oh, that's all right," Mrs Bishop said. "That's only Dally. He's the new gardener."

"So what was he doing over by the stables?"

Mrs Bishop shrugged. "Fetching some manure? Looking for tools? Have you finished down there? I'll get you a cup of coffee if you like."

"No, thank you. I've got to get back." Kirsty thought of the furtiveness of the young man's glance, the hurriedness of his walk. Why hadn't he said hello, even introduced himself? "Are you sure that's who it was?" she persisted. "He looked sort of guilty. As if he had no right to be here."

"No, that's him. He's a bit strange, Dally," Mrs Bishop said, "till you get used to him."

Cycling back to the yard to finish tidying and locking up, Kirsty glanced across the lawn and saw the boy working, digging the wide border by the walled garden. He didn't look at her.

CHAPTER 3

"The thing is," said Mrs Luckett, "Gemma really needs some better schooling fences, with the show season coming up. Couldn't you arrange something?"

Oh sure, Kirsty thought, I'll knock up a set of show jumps overnight, shall I, and build an indoor arena while I'm about it?

"There are some old hurdles, somewhere, and some oil drums," she said. "I'll look them out if you like."

Mrs Luckett looked sceptical. "It's not quite what I had in mind. Hardly what they're going to come across in the show ring. No, what we need is proper jumps, and a separate practice area where we can leave them out. There's that whole field doing nothing, on the other side of the lane. It wouldn't take much to put out a few markers."

"It's not doing nothing. It's *resting*," Kirsty explained patiently, "so that the grass can grow. If people start riding in there it'll get all churned up. Then there won't be any grass when we need it in a month or six weeks."

"But it'd only be used by Gemma and Alison." Mrs Luckett watched her daughter leading the grey pony out of the stable. "I know Alison agrees with me – she does a lot of competing, doesn't she? Riding-club events and suchlike. And for us, it's even more important. Petronella is an exceptional pony, and we're really hoping Gemma will do well with her this summer."

Kirsty, strongly suspecting who would get the blame if Gemma's success turned out to be less spectacular than Mrs Luckett imagined, eyed the pony's brand-new saddle and bridle with misgivings. The Lucketts had forked out enormous sums, for the pony herself – Nellie, as Kirsty and Jay called her – and then for every piece of equipment imaginable. It made Kirsty nervous, all this expensive stuff lying about in the tack-room. For security, there was just a flimsy hasp and a padlock. She would have to think about improvements.

"I know you're doing your best, dear," Mrs Luckett said in a friendlier tone. "But we may have to think about moving somewhere with better facilities. I can't have Gemma held back."

"I'll talk to Jay about it," Kirsty said quickly. The weekly cheque for Petronella, who was on full livery, added considerably to the yard's takings; she didn't want to have to tell Jay that the Nellies had gone elsewhere. Though if they went to one of the posher livery yards, like the one over at Wolverton, they'd end up paying double, at least. Gemma, who was about thirteen, wasn't too bad; Kirsty suspected that it was Mrs Luckett who fancied going to the shows in her Range Rover, bringing home trophies to polish. To her, the pony was a lifestyle accessory, a passport to the world of point-to-points and hunt balls.

Kirsty missed Jay. When he was around, they used to laugh privately about Mrs Luckett, whose accent was trying to move up the social scale, with occasional lapses into her native South London. Kirsty and Jay used to share tea and biscuits in the tack-room; they had mended gates and fences, and had marked out the schooling ring together, trying to work out from a copy of a Novice dressage test which way the letter-markers went. They had gone out riding together, Jay on excitable Leopardstown, Kirsty on the fat piebald, Patches, whose owner was happy for her to borrow him whenever she wanted. Jay, a gifted rider, had planned to take difficult horses for re-schooling. He was full of impressive ideas: getting sponsorship for eventing, bringing on young horses, buying more land from the neighbouring farmer, to extend the stables and build an indoor school. His latest venture – training for a year with an Olympic three-day-event rider in the States, working for his keep – seemed crazier than most. Kirsty couldn't quite reconcile Jay's big ambitions with what she saw in front of her – eight ramshackle stables in a yard where everything needed modernizing, mending or repainting, and tiles slid off the roofs every time there was a strong wind.

Now Kirsty had little time for riding, let alone for all the maintenance jobs. When Mrs Luckett and Gemma had taken their pony into the schooling field, she went indoors to make the shepherd's pie for supper. It was her turn to cook this week. She could leave it ready before cycling back to Ravenswood to fetch Prince in for the night.

It had been because of Jay and the horses that the family – when they *were* a family – had moved into Bramblings, left to them by Graham's grandparents. At first, he and Ursula thought they couldn't afford the upkeep; then Ursula had the idea of dividing the big Victorian house into two, selling half and investing the money. She had planned to restore and decorate their own part of the house, too; but then, last year, she and Kirsty's father had separated. Now, with Jay gone, only Kirsty and Graham were left, hardly a proper family at all. Some days, Kirsty hardly saw her father. At least Ursula, disliking horses, mud and mess, had good business sense, taking care of the orders and the accounts. Since last summer, Graham had taken no interest at all in the horses, owners or practical work, leaving it all to Jay, and now to Kirsty.

"Everything OK?" he asked her, while they ate the shepherd's pie at the kitchen table.

"Yes, thanks. Dorcas doesn't look near foaling yet. Mrs Nellie was moaning because we haven't got a set of show jumps."

"Stupid bloody woman," said Graham, though to Kirsty's knowledge he had never met Mrs Luckett. They ate in silence for a few moments. Nutmeg, the tabby cat, sat close to Graham's plate, watching every mouthful. Kirsty's mother would have been appalled at the idea of having cats in the house, let alone on the table, but Graham took no notice other than to give a vague swipe when Nutmeg looked too keenly interested. "You could have a look at my script after this," he said, "if you're not doing anything else."

"I've got to go round to Mrs Hendy's first. And finish off in the yard. Then I will."

It was almost dusk by the time Kirsty reached Ravenswood, a soft, spring dusk that breathed the scent of soil and new growth. A standard lamp was on in the front sitting-room, the room where Kirsty and Jay had been taken for sherry. Kirsty couldn't help glancing in. Mrs Hendy was sitting very upright on one of her velvet sofas, reading a book, the lamplight glossing her grey hair. Wasn't she afraid, alone in the huge house? Eventually, Jay had said, when Mrs Hendy died, her son would find the house too much of a burden and would sell it, for conversion into a country club or golfing hotel. Kirsty didn't like that, preferring to think of the garden as it was, deserted but for rabbits and blackbirds, the curve of lawn sweeping down to the unruffled surface of the lake.

She had forgotten her earlier fear until she rounded the bend to the stables and saw someone standing by the paddock gate. That boy. Dally.

He turned on hearing the crunch of tyres on gravel; again, she had an impression of boniness, of harshness in his face, of deep-set, intense eyes. Then he looked away, and stood as before, leaning on the top rail of the fence. He was looking at the horse, who raised his head from grazing and gave a fluttering whicker of greeting.

Slowly, Kirsty leaned her bike against the wall. The boy stayed where he was, ignoring her. She forked down straw in the stable, then unlocked the harness-room door and took out Prince's headcollar, reluctant to go up to the gate while the boy was standing there. If he was around all day, wouldn't it make sense for Mrs Hendy to ask him to bring the horse in for the night?

Why am I so awkward, Kirsty wondered? We're only two people. Why don't I just say "Hello!" in a perfectly normal, friendly way? Why doesn't he?

She walked up to the gate, trying to appear confident. He didn't turn again until she was right beside him.

"Hello!" she breezed. "I'm Kirsty. I look after Prince for Mrs Hendy. You're Dally, aren't you?" It sounded as fake as it was. Jolly-hockeysticks.

The boy looked at her quickly. He was tall and skinny, with that craggy face that made it hard to tell how old he was. Not really a boy – maybe twenty or so, she thought. His hair was straggly and needed washing, and the black jacket he wore was torn at the elbow – she could see his bent arm as he leaned against the fence, still gazing at Prince.

"I could do that," he said. His voice was hardly more than a mumble.

"What?"

"Get him in. Do all of it, the stable and all. Save you coming."

"I don't mind. I need the money," Kirsty said. Prince came up to her, pushing his nose into the headcollar. She smoothed her hand through the rough tangle of his mane. She ought to find time to groom him.

"Yeah, well, she's got plenty of that, the old bitch," Dally said.

Kirsty stared at him. Holding the headcollar rope, and with Prince snorting beside her, she felt more assured. "Do you work here all the time? Where do you live? I've never seen you around before."

"Wolverton. Near the bus station."

"Is Dally short for something?"

He shrugged. "Dallimore. My surname."

"Haven't you got a first name?"

"Dally. Just Dally."

"Dally Dallimore?" Kirsty looked at him as she led Prince through the churned gateway.

The boy didn't respond. He closed and bolted the gate, but didn't follow her to the stable. He stood watching from the fence while she led Prince into the stable, put on his night-rug, checked his water-bucket and fetched his feed from the store. He was making her feel edgy. He had been watching the horse – supposing he was planning to steal him, later? How much did Mrs Hendy know about him? She thought of the frail old lady reading in her sitting-room, with the curtains undrawn. Anyone could prowl round outside, and see her inside, alone and vulnerable. There must be all sorts of valuable things in the house – paintings, ornaments, furniture . . . money, credit cards. . .

"Bye, then," she called, when she had tidied everything away. "Are you going home now?"

Dally raised a hand and looked at her unsmiling. He stayed where he was.

Arriving back at Bramblings, she saw a red car parked in the yard. Tatjana, triumphant and glowing, was in the kitchen, sharing a bottle of wine with Kirsty's father. She let out a yelp as Kirsty came in and stood up, holding out both arms.

"I passed! Did you see my green L-plates?"

"Oh, well done!" Kirsty, who had forgotten all about Tat's test, went round the table and was crushed in an exuberant hug.

"First time! Brilliant, or what?" Tat smiled at Kirsty, releasing her. She smelled of freshly-washed hair and Calvin Klein perfume.

"Here, sit down. Let me get you a glass." Graham fetched one from the cupboard and sat down again, passing the filled glass to Kirsty. He raised his own. "To Tatjana! May the roads feel privileged to carry her in green-L-plated splendour."

Tat laughed and flicked her hair back, then drank deeply. Kirsty glanced at her father. He had got out of the habit of drinking this early in the evening; he said that it fuzzed his brain and stopped him from working, though she knew he sometimes drank whisky in his study, late, when she'd gone to bed. She asked Tat, "How long have you been here?"

"Only about ten minutes. I've got Mum's car for the evening and I was going to take you to the pub, but this is nice. Shall we go down later? Ross and Ollie might be there."

"I said I'd help Dad," Kirsty said. She could tell by his surprised expression that he'd forgotten. "I was going to read his script. Anyway, you can't drink and drive. Specially not on the day you pass your test."

"It doesn't matter, Mouse. About the script, I mean." Graham poured more wine for himself, then for Tat. "Not when Tatjana wants to celebrate. You might as well stay here and finish this off, then have some black coffee before you go. You'll be OK."

Mouse was Jay's nickname for Kirsty, from when she was little. It sounded odd, coming from her father, but she missed Jay so much that she liked hearing it. Graham always called Tat by her full name, Tatjana; a beautiful name, he had once said to Kirsty, mysterious, evocative of faded Russian aristocracy. No one would ever give Tatjana a nickname like Mouse. Tatjana was like her name – beautiful, a touch exotic, with long dark hair and a head-turning smile. Kirsty loved Tat, her best friend for years, but wished that fate had been more even-handed in the distribution of looks – she would have liked a share of Tatjana's beauty in exchange for her own pale, ordinary mouseness. It would be difficult not to be confident if you knew that people admired you wherever you went.

"How's it going, then? The writing?" Tat asked Graham, raising her glass.

"OK. I'm working fairly solidly now. My biggest problem is that all the main characters are in their late teens, London-based, into street life – difficult to get right when you're forty-four and living in a country backwater. That's why I want Kirsty to read what I've done so far."

"I know so much about trendy London people and drug trafficking, obviously," Kirsty said.

"Is that what it's about?" Tat asked. "What's it called?"

"*The Damage Done*," Graham told her. He raised his eyebrows, waiting to see what impact it made.

Tat thought for a moment, then said, "Oh, yeah, I get it. The old Neil Young song. 'The Needle and the Damage Done'." She hummed a phrase.

Graham smiled at her. "You know that?"

"My parents are a couple of old hippies. Neil Young's still a favourite of theirs. So tell me about your characters, then."

Kirsty sipped her wine and listened while her father outlined his ideas. He didn't usually talk much about his work; not to her. Their daily exchanges usually consisted of no more than "How's it going?" "Oh, not too bad, thanks." Tat, whose parents were a Russian historian and a lecturer in a sixth-form college, knew a bit about writing and publishing; her father wrote articles for learned academic journals, and gave lectures. Unlike Lottie, she wasn't thrown into stunned admiration by the fact that Kirsty's father had published novels. "Wow! You're a real writer! That's amazing!" Lottie had gushed, when she first found out. Kirsty knew that her father wasn't flattered by this kind of reaction, only irritated. Lottie, wrapped up in horses and competing and completely un-bookish, had the naive assumption that writers were automatically famous. Kirsty and her father knew better. Graham's three novels had had good reviews but hadn't sold well, and the first two had gone out of print. TV drama, he had decided now, was where big money could be made; he had set himself two months to write a script.

"What I liked in *The Darkness*," Tat was saying, "was the way you really got inside that girl's head. Irina's. I could really identify with her – she was totally convincing. I mean, if you can do that in fiction, you can surely do it in drama?"

"Perhaps. But it's all got to be more *oblique*," Graham said. "No narrative, no description – it's a completely different ball game, drama."

"But you can do brilliant dialogue," Tat said. "If you can do that, and create great characters, then that's a pretty good start, surely? It's down to the actors to do the rest."

Tatjana had actually read all three of Kirsty's father's novels, read them properly, which gave her far more credit with him than any amount of misplaced awe. Kirsty never felt that she could read them herself with any sort of detachment. They made her uneasy. One reason was the sex – in anybody else's book she would have read those scenes with a different kind of close attention, but here she couldn't shake off her awareness that this was Dad's writing. He knew about lurid and, to Kirsty's mind, sometimes disgusting things that people did to each other. He must have done it all, and not only with Mum. She didn't want to think about that.

"What would be really helpful," Graham said to Tat, "would be if you'd *both* have a look at the script, you and Kirsty. Tell me what you think. Honestly."

"Oh, I'd love to! What, now? Here?"

Kirsty was beginning to feel like an unwanted third in this conversation. She looked at the two of them, facing each other across the table: Tat, vivacious and animated, a hand raised to push back her hair; Graham, inclined towards her, his eyes on her face while he talked, barely remembering to flick an occasional glance at Kirsty. They were a pair of charmers, charming each other. With Tat, it was unintentional; she was like this with everyone. With Dad—

She stood up.

"Come on," she said curtly to Tat. "Let's go up to my room. We can read up there. Don't let us stop you from working, Dad."

CHAPTER 4

For once, Kirsty had made her bed and left her room reasonably tidy. The tabby cat, Nutmeg, had settled herself on the duvet, curled like a dormouse. She opened her visible eye just a slit, not bothering to move. Kirsty sat on the bed and picked hayseeds off her socks, wondering whether she smelled of horses and stables.

Tat, roaming around the room with her wine-glass still in her hand, took down a book from the shelves. Kirsty saw at a glance what it was: *Foxtail*, by Graham Millen. Dad's second novel. Tat turned it over to look at Graham's photograph on the back, the one from six years ago that made him look brooding and pensive, heavy-browed.

"He's so *hands*ome, your dad!" Tat said.

That photo had made him look older than he was, so that in real life he had just about caught up. Kirsty knew by heart what it said on the back cover: the blurb, the bit about him being a talented newcomer, and the quotation from a *Guardian* review of his first book that said he showed *a sharp, uncanny insight into adolescent angst.*

"It's just that photo," Kirsty said. "Good lighting."

"No, it's not! I've seen him in the flesh, haven't I?"

"Tell me about the driving test," Kirsty said. "Didn't you do *any*thing stupid?"

Tat giggled, sliding the book back into place. She wasn't usually a giggler; it must be the wine, Kirsty thought, grabbing at a handy excuse not to go to the pub later.

"Well, there was one bit, in the middle of the three-point-turn," Tat said, "when I put the hand-brake on really hard, to make sure the instructor saw me doing it. Only I did it so hard that I couldn't let it off again! Honestly, I was about to ask him to do it for me – I'd have felt a right dork, but then I gave a stupendous heave, just in time. Anyway, isn't it great? We'll be able to go out now without bothering anyone for lifts – Mum hardly ever uses her car Friday or Saturday nights." Tat sprawled on the bed next to Kirsty. "This Saturday, for a start. Everyone's going round to Ollie's – he told me to tell you. Bring a bottle."

"Oh, I can't," Kirsty said automatically. "Sorry."

"Why not? You never go *any*where these days, as far as I can see."

The sick feeling curdled in Kirsty's stomach. She stroked Nutmeg's ear. "I do. I do go out."

"Oh? You do?" Tat sat up, hugging her knees. "Have you met someone?"

Kirsty smoothed her hand along the cat's warm striped body. "Yes. Actually I have. His name's Adam and he's the son of Dad's girlfriend – you know, Clare. He's home from Warwick and he's gorgeous. And intelligent. And funny."

"And you're going *out* with him? Since when?"

"Not exactly going out. He's away at university most of the time. We e-mail each other."

"An e-mail romance! And now you're about to meet again in person? When do I get to meet him? Can't you bring him on Saturday?"

"No, I can't. We're going over to Clare's for lunch."

"That won't take all day! You can come to Ollie's later on! Does Adam drive? Has he got a car?"

"No. Look, Tat. You won't say anything to Dad about this, will you? He doesn't know yet – promise?"

"Mysteriouser and mysteriouser!" Tat said delightedly. "So how did the two of you get together without him knowing?"

"Oh – there are ways. Come on. That's enough about him. I thought we were going to read Dad's script?"

"Yeah, let's." Tat sat up, reached for the printed pages, then looked at Kirsty in puzzlement. "Wait – if you and Adam e-mail each other, how do you stop your dad from seeing the messages? He's the one who uses the computer all the time, isn't he?"

"Oh—" For a second Kirsty thought of telling the truth, but instead she said: "I trash them. Adam always mails first thing in the morning, and I trash the messages as soon as I've read them."

Tatjana giggled. "I'd no idea you were so sly. So thoroughly devious!"

Kirsty looked away. Sometimes she surprised herself, finding out just how sly and devious she could be. For most of the time, she had stopped noticing.

Lying to Tat – lying to everyone – had become a habit.

Kirsty knew exactly when it had started – early last June, on the last day of her GCSE exams. She had felt sick before each of the exams, but had kept herself under control; she could manage, as long as she was near the back of the hall. Then the last day. French in the morning, History in the afternoon. And by some quirk of the alphabet she found herself sitting at the front of the hall, at the head of the middle row, for the French exam.

"French candidates, you can begin."

And the hall was a-flutter with the opening of question papers. Kirsty, trying to read the questions, was conscious only of the silence pressing against her ears, of the breathing rows of people behind her, of the squeak of a shoe against the gym floor. No one else seemed to be having trouble breathing. In, out. In, out. The more she concentrated on getting air in and out of her, the less she seemed to get. Air, in the stuffy gym, had turned into a thick, glutinous substance like treacle; it clogged her throat, not reaching her lungs. *Kirsty Millen*, she had written on her paper, and that was all, while the hand of the big clock fastened to the wall-bars swept away the minutes. Then, a footfall close to her, a waft of perfume, and the flowered skirt of one of the supervising teachers brushed past her. Kirsty glimpsed a sandalled foot with toe-nails painted dark red. The teacher, one of the Modern Language staff whose name Kirsty didn't know, turned and stood at the front of the gym, arms folded, in a curiously military posture that was at odds with her light summer clothes. In, out. In, out. Kirsty stared at the yellow exam paper and willed oxygen into her lungs.

You have arranged to spend a fortnight with your French penfriend in Paris. . . Your friend has sent you this letter about plans for the visit. . . The words spiralled in front of her, no longer anchored to the page. French words butted into her head, hundreds of meaningless sounds pronouncing themselves at once, all the words she had spent so long cramming in last night. Her head couldn't hold it, without oxygen. *Kirsty Millen*, she read on her answer paper, a random collection of vowels and consonants. How odd to think that those black marks meant her. *Milly Kirsten, Misty Curtain* – the words danced and blurred. She imagined herself blacking out, toppling to the floor, and everyone else carrying on with their exam, not noticing. At the end, the teacher collecting the papers would step over her slumped body. . .

In a tremor of panic she shoved back her chair and stumbled to her feet, accidentally sweeping her exam paper to the floor. Surprised faces gaped as she bolted down the narrow aisle between desks. She saw miniature teddy mascots and lucky dice key-rings and pocket French dictionaries; pens moving over paper, producing script like rows of knitting. Tat mouthed something at her; she glimpsed Ross's anxious face. Reaching the double doors, Kirsty pushed past another teacher who held out a hand to restrain her. She burst out to the deserted corridor, where notices warned: *Silence – exam in progress.*

The teacher was following her through the swing doors. Gulping air, Kirsty ran the length of the corridor, turned a corner, turned again into the caretaker's area and out into the air.

Free.

Later, when Mr Bricknell, the exam secretary, phoned home, she said she had felt sick. Had to rush to the loo. No time to put her hand up, to explain.

Why hadn't she come back to continue the exam? Mr Bricknell wanted to know. Why hadn't she told someone? Where had she gone? The invigilating teacher had looked for her in the girls' toilets nearest the gym—

She was ill, Kirsty insisted. Sick. Must have eaten something – couldn't stop throwing up. That seemed to excuse everything. There had been only one place to go. She had cycled home, straight to the stable-yard to find Jay, and collapsed in a storm of weeping.

"Hey, Mouse! What's happened?"

He was in the sunlit yard, in jeans and T-shirt, hosing Leo's swollen tendon, while collared doves pecked at spilled grain and both cats basked by a wall. Kirsty smelled Leo's warm coat, and the hay and the dust of the yard, and couldn't explain. Not even to Jay, who put his arm round her and soothed her and eventually, when he couldn't get any sense out of her, left her sitting on an upturned bucket, while he went to fetch their mother from the house.

Ursula, who had come back to Bramblings for the day to finish packing up her stuff, was brisk and practical. "Are you quite sure you can't go back? All right then, have a rest now, and I'll drive you back for the History this afternoon. Fetch you again afterwards, if you like. It's your GCSEs, Kirsty, your future! You'll have to make the effort!"

No. Nothing was going to make Kirsty go back into that exam hall. There were phone calls, Mum to Mr Bricknell, Mr Bricknell to Kirsty. She wouldn't fail her exams outright, it seemed. There were allowances for illness, for special circumstances. She would get something based on her teachers' estimated grades and the papers she had already done.

Tatjana phoned at lunchtime, on her mobile. "What happened to you? You looked like you'd seen a ghost. You're coming back for History, aren't you?"

Kirsty didn't. Not that day, nor since.

It was amazingly easy, she found, once she'd started to lie, to carry on doing it. People were so gullible. She felt sick. She didn't like parties. She was too busy to go shopping in town; too tired, too skint for the pub or the cinema. No one suspected, not even Tat.

"Hey, you're not *pregnant*, are you?" Tat said, when Kirsty missed the year eleven leavers' party.

"Don't be daft," Kirsty scoffed.

But she hadn't known then, for certain, that she wasn't. She knew why Ross had looked anxious; it was more on his own behalf than hers. A week later, the familiar dragging ache proved that particular worry groundless.

The other fears remained, grew stronger. They thumped her into wakefulness in mid-dream; they tingled in the silent darkness. They buzzed in her ears, threatening to speak inside her head. What, exactly, she was afraid of, she couldn't have said: she was frightened of being frightened. Afraid of her own mind and what it might produce to terrify her.

Jay was the only person she could have told. Several times, she stood by his bedroom door, hesitated, heard his steady breathing – sometimes, gentle snoring – and tiptoed away again. In the yard, or out riding with him, she rehearsed her confession: "Jay, I think I'm going mad."

But Jay had flown out to the States without knowing his sister was insane. He was so unsuspecting that he left her to look after his most prized possession, his horse; he left her in charge of his business. Jay had met Emma: sleek, assured Emma, with her perfect American teeth and her flawless skin and her Bronx accent. He talked incessantly about Emma, what Emma said, what Emma thought. When he came back from a weekend with her, full of excitement at the idea of going to Connecticut, Kirsty knew she would have to manage without him. For a whole year. Jay had left in September, which had at least given Kirsty the excuse she needed to avoid going back to school.

"You can come out and stay, Mouse!" Jay had promised her. "I'll take you sightseeing in New York. Bloomingdales, the Empire State Building, Central Park – you'll love it!"

The Empire State Building, the lift crammed with people, the long ascent – Kirsty shuddered. But she had kept her secrets successfully enough to fool even him.

Morning, and the weather had turned colder, as if spring was regretting its impulsiveness of the last few days. Kirsty wore her fleece jacket zipped right up to the neck, and felt the wind cold through her jeans as she fed the horses before breakfast. It was Good Friday. The next few days would be busy, with all the livery owners off work for the Easter weekend; she did all the stables and left the yard tidy before she went in for breakfast. Afterwards, Ravenswood, and then she would groom Petronella, and clean the tack she should have done last night.

She cycled the half-mile to Mrs Hendy's. Beside the track, near the vegetable beds and the garden sheds that were hidden from the house by a yew hedge, there was a big heap of garden waste – prunings and dead twigs – from the work the strange boy had done yesterday. He was going to have a bonfire, presumably. Kirsty half-expected him to be hanging round the stables again, or to startle her with a sudden appearance. Only when she was putting Prince's headcollar back in the harness-room did she notice that the bolt on the hatchway to the loft had been left open. She stood frowning at it. She was sure she had closed it yesterday, and locked the harness-room door behind her.

Maybe he was up there now.

She thought of the way he had hung around last night, remembered his unsmiling stare. Mrs Bishop ought to know.

Purposefully, Kirsty cycled up to the house. Finding the back door ajar, she went in without ringing the bell. Mrs Bishop was talking to someone in the kitchen; Kirsty knocked on the door and pushed it open, expecting to find Mrs Hendy there.

"Excuse me, but –"

"Yes, dear? Come on in and have some tea – it's a bit nippy out there."

Kirsty stared. They were sitting at the big kitchen table, two of them. Mrs Bishop, with a chopping board and knife and a heap of carrots; the boy, Dally, eating toast.

"Oh," Kirsty said.

They both had mugs of tea in front of them. Mrs Bishop looked far more agreeable than she had yesterday; as if they'd just been sharing a good old gossip and joke, her and the boy. Kirsty couldn't imagine it. Again she noticed Dally's deep-set, shadowed eyes, and his hawkish face. He didn't look like someone who smiled much.

"I'll just put some more hot water in the pot," said Mrs Bishop, standing. "You know Dally, don't you?"

"Yes."

Dally flicked a glance at Kirsty, with a grunting sound that might have meant Hello. He carried on eating his toast, sitting with hunched shoulders as if someone might snatch the plate away.

"Shall I put some more toast on?" Mrs Bishop offered. "You going to sit down and warm yourself up for a bit?"

"No, I've got to go. And no tea, thanks," Kirsty said.

"What did you want, then, dear?"

"Oh – er –" Kirsty faltered.

Then Mrs Bishop clapped a hand over her mouth. "Your money! It's Friday, isn't it? You mustn't be too shy to ask, dear. I clean forgot – I'll draw some out later. Can you come back for it this evening?"

And Kirsty agreed, feeling thoroughly mercenary.

CHAPTER 5

It felt weird to be riding again; even weirder to be riding Leo, who was 16.3 hands and narrow, and made Kirsty feel she was perched on top of a racehorse. He was so tall that she had to use the mounting block in the yard to get into the saddle. Jay, tall and athletic, could vault up; for Kirsty, only five foot four, mounting from ground level was a stretch more than she could manage.

Examining his injured tendon earlier and finding it not puffy at all, she had decided to start giving him quiet exercise. She would start with half-an-hour's walking each day, then, if the tendon remained unswollen, build up to more, so that when Jay returned in September he would find his horse halfway to being fit again. Quiet exercise may have been what Kirsty intended, but Leo, not having been ridden out for months, was skittish and excitable: he shied at sparrows in the hedge, snatched at the bit, veered close to the ditch that ran beside the lane. Kirsty had ridden him a few times before, but only in the schooling field, and with Jay present. She soothed him, sitting quietly, hoping he would settle. Then, just as she persuaded him to walk sensibly, hoofbeats clattered round the bend in the lane and a black pony appeared at a fast trot. Kirsty had time to recognize Lottie and her black Welsh cob before Leo plunged and half-reared, trying to whirl round. Kirsty steadied him, turned him and made him walk forward.

Lottie had pulled up in a gateway. "Wow! I thought it was Jay, for a minute. Are you OK?"

"Yes, thanks," Kirsty gasped. "He's just a bit excited, out for the first time."

"You look great on him! Where are you going?"

"Half-an-hour's quiet exercise. Supposedly."

"I'll come with you," Lottie offered. "He'll be quieter, with Puzzle. I was just coming over to see you anyway. Never thought you'd be out riding." She turned her pony to take the lead. With the stolid cob ahead of him, Leo stopped fretting and walked calmly; Kirsty patted his neck. Lottie, turning in her saddle, said, "Actually something horrible's happened. I came to tell you."

"Oh no, what?" Kirsty imagined some disaster on the small farm run by Lottie's father, who had had a stroke two years ago.

"The police came round early this morning. There's been an attack on a horse at Wolverton Stud, a brood mare. Stabbed, out in a field."

"No! Stabbed – you don't mean *killed*?"

"No, not killed. Injured by some maniac. She'll be OK – so will the foal. But the police wanted to warn us, and ask if we've seen anything suspicious. I expect they'll ask you, too.

Isn't it horrible? I mean, you read about these things, horses being attacked, but I mean, *here* –"

Kirsty looked at Puzzle's plump hindquarters, his thick plumy tail, his hooves treading the gritty dust at the side of the lane. She thought of someone creeping up on him in his field, knife in hand, with the intention of wounding and hurting; imagined her own hand grasping the knife, her senses burning with some uncontrollable anger.

If you could do that, what could you not do?

"What can we do?" she asked Lottie. "Did the police say anything? We can't keep the horses in, can we? And even if we did, they'd be just as vulnerable in their stables –" Anxiety tugged at her. "And I've got the two fillies, the Anglo-Arabs, turned out in the bottom field. I check them every day, but –"

Lottie turned to rest a hand on the back of her saddle. Her blonde pony-tail rippled down her back. "Keep a look-out for anyone strange, they said. And I suppose they – I mean the police – they'll be around more, now this has happened."

Anyone strange, Kirsty thought. Dally.

"You haven't seen anyone, I suppose?" she asked Lottie.

"No – I mean no one comes out our way, except to deliver cattle feed or something like that. That's one good thing, we can't be seen from the road. Have you?"

"No," Kirsty said. She thought of Prince, alone in his small paddock, screened from the house by the yew hedge. She thought of Dally, standing by the gate staring at him. "Do you mind if we go round to Mrs Hendy's?" she asked Lottie. "I just want to check Prince – you know I'm looking after him now? You've got me a bit neurotic, telling me all this."

Apart from Leo snorting with great suspicion at the postman's bike and prancing like a Lipizzaner stallion, they reached Ravenswood without incident. "If you wait here, I'll just have a quick look," Kirsty said by the gates. She slithered to the ground, wondering how she was going to get up again, and passed Leo's reins to Lottie. She didn't want to startle Mrs Hendy by taking both horses past the house. "I won't be a minute."

Unless—

She didn't want to think of what she might see. Of what that brood mare's owner must have seen, first thing this morning.

As she ran to the stables, she heard, to her vast relief, Prince neighing, and Leo's deep-throated whinny in reply. The stable-yard was deserted. Prince trotted to the gate, head high, eyes straining for a glimpse of the other horses. He was lonely, bored. Nothing had been disturbed in the yard, and there was no sign of Dally.

"Good boy." Kirsty patted his dusty neck. "I'll come back for you soon."

She hurried back to Lottie, between the yew hedges, and saw that Lottie wasn't alone. A wheelbarrow, loaded with twigs and prunings, stood on the gravel track and Lottie was talking to Dally, who was holding Leo's reins and stroking him.

Kirsty stopped dead, taking in the scene as if reading a tableau: Lottie smiling, sitting loosely in her saddle, with her hair falling over one shoulder; Puzzle eating the long grass on the verge; Leo resting his nose on Dally's shoulder, while the boy stroked – no, scratched, gently – his cheek. Leo's eyelids drooped; he nuzzled Dally's shoulder.

She marched up to the horse and took the reins. "Here, give him to me."

Dally looked at her, startled, and stepped back.

"It's all right, he was just helping," Lottie said. "Leo got a bit neurotic when he heard the neighing. But he's fine now."

For the second time that day, Kirsty felt herself wrong-footed by Dally. He had certainly had a calming effect on Leo. For a horse just described as neurotic, the big bay was standing as placidly as a seaside donkey.

"Thanks," she said to Dally. It came out grudgingly. She looked up at the saddle and wondered whether to let down the stirrup. It would be an ungainly struggle, mounting, and she didn't want to look ungainly in front of Dally.

"Here," Dally said. He came and stood beside Leo's shoulder and bent to give her a leg-up. She wondered if he knew how to do it; then felt herself thrown lightly up and into the saddle.

"Thanks," she said again, looking down at Dally from her superior height. She collected up her reins with a great show

44

of proficiency, pushed her feet into the stirrups and clicked her tongue to wake Leo up.

"Bye!" Lottie called to Dally, as they rode on. Surreptitiously, Kirsty looked back over her shoulder. He was still standing there, watching them.

"Have you seen him before?" she asked Lottie, when they were out of earshot.

"No. He works for Mrs Hendy, does he? He seems pretty good with horses."

"What were you talking about?" Kirsty didn't see how it was possible to have a conversation with Dally; she had only ever heard him communicate in monosyllables or grunts.

"Oh, he was asking about the horses. Whether they were both mine. I told him no, if he'd seen our ramshackle place he'd never expect to see a classy horse like Leo there."

An iced-water shiver trickled down Kirsty's back. "You didn't tell him where you *live?*"

"Well yes, why – ?"

"Lottie, are you mad? Have you already forgotten what we were talking about? Strange people hanging round, your place out of sight from the road?"

Lottie's eyes widened. "You don't mean you think he's the one who attacked that mare? But he's good with horses – you saw for yourself."

Yes, Kirsty had. She had seen, in the instant before she intervened, the boy's face close to the horse's, his expression absorbed, even tender. Most boys would have been looking at Lottie, with her sturdy English-rose prettiness, all smiles and curves and tumbling blonde hair, but this one had definitely been more interested in the horse. And Kirsty did not find that reassuring.

"Yes, I know, but does that make it any less likely?" she pointed out. "Those people who hurt horses, out in fields, they'd have to know something about them, surely? How to approach them? Not everyone could do it."

"But why *him*? Do you know him? Anything about him?"

"No – I only met him yesterday. Not really met – just saw. He was hanging round Prince's paddock. I don't know how long he's been working there. Jay never said anything about him."

"Well, I thought he seemed quite nice." Lottie gave Kirsty a defiant look.

"*Nice –*"

"Coming up and helping like that, when he saw I was in trouble. Honestly, Leo nearly pulled my arm out of its socket. Another few seconds and I'd have been on the floor. He didn't say anything or make a fuss, just came up from behind the bushes and got hold of the reins. That's not the sort of thing that happens to me every day," Lottie said, with a whimsical smile. "Rescued by strange young men—"

"For God's sake, Lottie, you'll have him in shining armour next! Sir Lancelot or something. Just remember, we don't know the first thing about him, and *strange* is probably the right word. That housekeeper said so, Mrs Bishop. 'He's a bit strange, Dally, till you get to know him.' That's what she said."

"Dally? And he's Mrs Hendy's gardener?" Lottie asked. "A proper gardener? Does he know how to do things with dahlias and delphiniums?"

"Odd-job person, I should think, more likely. I mean, you'd have to know an awful lot about gardening, wouldn't you, to run a place the size of that? I've only seen him clearing stuff, the sort of thing anyone could do. Anyway he only looks about twenty, wouldn't you say?"

They had looped round, through the village, past the pub and the church. The two sets of hooves echoed between the house walls in the main street. Leo was walking calmly now, on a long rein, not spooking even when someone slammed the hatch of an estate car outside the shop.

"I bet he's a student, or taking a year out," Lottie said. "Or maybe earning a bit of money so that he can do something really interesting. I bet he's an artist, or an author like your dad. Anyway, you can find out, can't you? You're up there twice a day."

"I'm not sure I want to find out," Kirsty said.

"I've been out riding with Lottie," she told her father when she took him up a mug of tea. "She's downstairs, now."

"Good." He wasn't really listening. If it had been Tatjana, he'd have come down to join them in the kitchen, but he wasn't interested in Lottie. He always called her "that horsey

47

female". They were so amazingly different, Kirsty's two friends – Tattie and Lottie, as Jay called them – that she made efforts to ensure that they never met each other. Tat was intellectual, Lottie completely unacademic; Tat was worldly and well-informed, a *Guardian* reader like her parents, while Lottie only read *Horse and Hound* or *Farmer's Weekly*, like hers. Tat intended to read English at university and become a journalist; Lottie helped her father on the farm and her mother with two younger children, and was half-heartedly attending a cookery course at Newington College, with the vague aim of getting work as a chalet girl or au pair until she found someone to marry. "All I want is someone really nice, who looks like Tim Henman, and he must be reasonably well-off, and like skiing, and have his own Welsh Cob stud. Is that too much to ask?"

Kirsty wasn't sure where Lottie could hope to find a partner meeting these precise specifications. Meanwhile, as she had just proved, she was prepared to show interest in someone who didn't match a single one of them. The person Lottie would really like to marry was Jay, whom she openly adored, but since Emma had entered Jay's life she was having to make do with a catering student who modelled himself on Jamie Oliver.

Riding out, and having tea with Lottie, had made Kirsty late. She fed the horses, checked the fillies in the bottom field – so far out of sight from the road, she decided, that they were probably safer there than anywhere else – brought

Dorcas in and checked her for signs of imminent foaling. Then she went in to cook, deciding to leave Prince till after.

"So what did she – what did you think?" Graham asked, over the meal.

"About what?"

"Tatjana. About the script."

"Oh." Kirsty wasn't surprised to notice whose opinion really mattered. "She liked it. We both did. Tat liked Nadia, especially – a strong character, she said – and the way you set up the clash between her and her father in the first scene."

"Mmm?" Graham, with his mouth full, waved his fork in a circle, prompting her to say more. He wouldn't be satisfied until he got a word-for-word account of Tatjana's response.

"Oh, by the way," Kirsty said, when she had exhausted the subject and passed on Tatjana's two small criticisms. "Lottie told me about an attack on a horse in a field. A brood mare, stabbed, in a field over at Wolverton. The police came round, she said." Her father spent long hours sitting at his desk, staring out of his study window – he might, possibly, notice if a stranger came down the lane, or an unfamiliar vehicle was parked.

"Yes, I know." Graham stirred his coffee. "They phoned while you were out. I said you'd ring them back if you knew anything."

Kirsty gave him a hard, disbelieving stare. "What, and you didn't think it was important enough to mention?"

He looked at her mildly. "Well, you knew about it. You've just told me."

"That's not the point! I might *not* have known! And you couldn't even be bothered to tell me!" She got up from the table and clattered dishes in the sink, then wondered why she was bothering. "For God's sake, Dad, you're so incredibly self-centred! Your precious script, that's all that matters – the horses could be slaughtered out in the field for all you care!"

"Don't be ridiculous! Of course I would have told you. We were talking about something else, that's all."

"I'm going out." She went to the back door and pulled on her boots.

"Where to?"

"Up to Mrs Hendy's. There's a weird bloke hanging round up there, but don't bother yourself."

She slammed the door behind her. The washing-up would still be there in the sink when she got back; she knew that for certain.

CHAPTER 6

In the long shadows of early evening, Kirsty cycled to Ravenswood. Riding Leo, and even the argument with her father, had made her feel more confident, more assertive. She was looking forward to riding again; tomorrow, when she could get at Graham's computer, she would send an e-mail to Jay, a long one, to tell him about it. Should she tell him about the attack on the mare, and the police phone call? She wanted his advice, his reassurance; but perhaps it would be unfair to worry him over something he could do nothing about.

When Jay left, she had done her best to prepare for any kind of emergency that might throw itself at her. She read books and books about horse care, learning about illnesses with fearsome names like strangles and azoturia; she watched the horses obsessively, convinced they would all develop alarming symptoms the instant Jay was out of the country. One consolation was that Lottie's mother had been a riding-instructress years ago, and Lottie herself had been reared on Pony Club rallies and tests and all sorts of horse know-how. Between them, they would advise her, come round if necessary. She had the vet's phone number pinned on the cork board in the kitchen, together with numbers for the black-smith and the feed merchant and the saddler, her back-up team. But attacks were violent and unpredictable, and likely to happen at night, when no one could help. She thought again about the two Anglo-Arab fillies. Were they safer where they were? Should she bring them up to the small paddock near the yard, over-grazed though it was?

The day had softened, the sun making a late appearance and the wind dying down to a faint breeze. There were bright flowers in the churchyard – a few early bluebells and frail wood anemones under the trees, and, by some of the graves, the brasher colours of tulips or hot-house roses, some still wrapped in their cellophane. It was still Good Friday. On the noticeboard beside the lych-gate, a poster announced the times of Easter services, beneath a crude sketch of a crucified figure. It was a familiar enough image to demand little attention, yet Kirsty slowed to look. A more horrible form of torture it would be hard to imagine, she thought – yet this had been imagined, and carried out, done not just to Jesus but routinely. In the village shop window there were Easter eggs, coloured streamers and fake daffodils. A strange mixture, this weekend: torture and fluffy chicks, slow death and chocolate eggs wrapped in ribbon. Again Kirsty felt a shiver of revulsion at the thought that someone could invade this quiet village, *her* village, with violence and cruelty.

No. She rode on, making herself think more positive thoughts. She wasn't going to start frightening herself now.

She waved to Mr Simpkins, who was walking his Labrador, and summoned her capable, efficient self. Half an hour to do Prince; then home, a hot bath and some television before bed. Out with Mum, tomorrow – she wasn't looking forward to that. She found herself remembering the ridiculous lies she'd told Tatjana, about Adam. Now, she could hardly believe that she'd been so stupid – it must have been the wine. What now? Should she tell Tat that she'd made it all up? Or would it be simpler to meet this wretched Adam, just once, get his e-mail address, and make at least part of it come true?

The stone frontage of Ravenswood was washed in late sunlight, looking less forbidding than usual. A magnolia bush on the front lawn was still in flower, its ivory petals curved and gleaming. There was no lamp lit in the large corner room, but as Kirsty cycled past, she heard a rapping on the window and saw Mrs Hendy standing there, beckoning for her to come in. Kirsty leaned her bike against the wall and went round to the pillared entrance. She heard Mrs Hendy's slow footsteps approaching, the click of her heeled shoes on hard flooring, then the door was unlocked from inside. Kirsty was rather relieved that Mrs Hendy did keep the door locked, although it wasn't yet late.

"Hello, Kirsty." Mrs Hendy wasn't the sort to say *dear* or *love*. She had the sort of smile that was more like a ritual baring of teeth. "Mrs Bishop told me you were coming back for your money, so I had it ready."

"I've come back to bring Prince in," Kirsty said. "I'm a bit late, tonight."

The old lady didn't answer. Behind her, Kirsty saw the dark tiled hallway, with a huge sideboard, a Chinese vase and various brass candlesticks. Mrs Hendy took some notes from a saucer on the sideboard and handed them to her.

"There, thirty-five pounds. I like to pay my debts on time. Is everything all right?"

"Yes," Kirsty said, uncertainly.

Mrs Hendy looked at her closely. "You don't sound too sure. Have you got too much to do, with your brother away? It's a lot of responsibility for you."

"No – it's fine. I like it. I was just wondering – that gardener, Dally, has he worked here long?"

"A couple of weeks. I put an advert in the local paper and he answered it. Why do you ask?"

"I thought I recognized him from somewhere," Kirsty improvised.

"Well, he's a good worker, I'll say that for him. I won't keep you now, as it's late, but come in and have a sherry next time."

Kirsty put the notes in the back pocket of her jeans, collected her bike and went on to the stables. Evidently, she thought, the police hadn't phoned Mrs Hendy yet – maybe they didn't realize she kept a horse. Kirsty hadn't wanted to alarm her, but maybe she should have mentioned it. She led

Prince into the stable, measured out his feed and fetched the grooming brushes to clean him up a bit before putting on his night rug. The evening was so pleasant that she felt in no hurry to go home, especially after her outburst with her father. She brushed dust and loose hair from Prince's coat, soothed by the sound of his eating and the warm stable smells. Over the half-door of his stable, she could see across his paddock to the fields by the river. The hedgerows were frosted with blackthorn blossom; at the wood's edge, in the direction of Bramblings, a flowering cherry was like a ghost tree against the starker outlines of those not yet in leaf. A thrush sang somewhere close, repeating each snatch of melody.

When she heard footsteps on gravel, and Dally looked in at her over the door, she wasn't as nervous as she would have been earlier. No one besides her seemed to find him in the least threatening. Prince, intent on his food, didn't even look up from the manger.

"Thought you weren't coming," he said, looking at her directly. It sounded as if he'd been waiting for her.

She carried on brushing dried mud off Prince's stomach, bending to see. "I'm a bit late tonight. What about you? Aren't you going home?"

"Soon."

"How do you get home? You don't drive, do you?"

"I walk."

Kirsty looked at him in surprise. Wolverton was a good

five miles – not too far to walk, but far enough before and after a day's work.

"You work long hours," she said.

He shrugged. "I like it here."

"Better than home?" she asked. It was gone seven; surely Mrs Hendy didn't expect him to stay so late. Maybe he was going to the pub, meeting someone for the evening. Dally didn't answer. His face was in shadow; she couldn't see his expression. About to ask who he lived with, she thought better of it. She started to brush out Prince's tail.

"Thanks for helping with Leo this afternoon," she said.

"You looked different, riding him. Snooty. Like that posh blonde girl you were with."

"I'm not posh, neither's Lottie. She just sounds it."

"Lottie," he sneered. "Posh name. Kirsty's all right. Nice. Scottish?"

"My grandmother is." Kirsty moved round to Prince's other side, taking her time. When she'd finished, she'd have to leave the stable, push past Dally.

"He's fantastic, that horse," Dally said.

"Prince?"

"I meant the one you were riding. Yours?"

"No! I couldn't afford a horse like Leo. He belongs to my brother. Do you ride?"

"*Do you ride?*" he mimicked, making her sound posh, a snooty horsey girl. "No, I don't ride. Don't want to. The way you boss them about, with your bits and spurs and whips – they don't need it. Don't deserve it."

"I didn't *have* spurs, or a whip!" Kirsty retorted. "You make me sound like a lion-tamer!"

Dally shrugged. The light was fading; it was dim in the stable and she could no longer see his face. She crossed to the door and flicked on the light switch. Dally didn't move aside; he stayed leaning on the top of the door frame, resting his chin on his crossed arms. His eyes followed her as she went back to Prince. Kirsty thought: I don't care what Lottie says, or Mrs Hendy. He's creepy, and I don't like him being here. Prince gave a deep, contented sigh into his manger, sending up a spray of oat husks and chaff.

"That horse," he said, "that Leo, he could easily throw you off if he wanted to, or bolt. You wouldn't be able to stop him."

"No," Kirsty said. "I know."

"Why do they put up with it?" Dally asked. "Why do they let you order them about? Do this, walk like this, jump that – what gives anyone the right?"

Kirsty finished brushing, put the brush in the plastic carrier and threw Prince's night-rug over his back. "Look," she said, while she fastened the buckles and the surcingle, "I don't know what point you're making, but what I do know is that I spend my whole life looking after horses – my brother's and Mrs Hendy's and other people's. I look after them as well as I possibly can and do everything for them and I'd never hurt them. Horses are expensive – people can't keep them as pets. OK, they get ridden – that doesn't seem specially cruel to me. All these horses have pretty luxurious lives compared to lots of people in Kosovo, if you ask me, or Ethiopia. I've finished now and I'm going home."

She had impressed herself with this speech. It silenced Dally, who said no more while she straightened the rug, picked up the grooming kit and headcollar and put them away in the harness-room. She locked up and put the key in her pocket. Prince, his meal finished, moved to the door and lifted his head over, pushing his nose into Dally's chest.

"I'll help, if you want," he said, as Kirsty fetched her bike.

"Help what? I've just told you, I'm going home. I've finished."

"At your place, I mean. While your brother's away."

Kirsty, about to say, *And how do you know my brother's away?* realized that Mrs Bishop must have told him. She would have preferred Dally not to know that. What else did he know?

"No, thanks," she said curtly. "I can manage."

Kirsty phoned Lottie when she got home, but Lottie had gone out with the Jamie Oliver clone.

"Everything all right?" Graham came in to the kitchen. "I heard you come back. You were a long time, weren't you?"

"Mrs Hendy called me in for a chat," Kirsty said shortly.

"I was starting to get worried," Graham said. He put the kettle on and started to make coffee.

"There's a first time for everything."

He touched her arm. "Look, I'm sorry about that phone call. Not telling you straight away. It's just that I—"

"Yes, I know, you had your mind on higher things. Your Art," Kirsty said caustically. "You're out all day tomorrow, aren't you?"

"Yes, I told you."

Kirsty wasn't happy at the thought of leaving the yard unsupervised for a couple of hours at lunchtime. Admittedly, she left it every day, while she went to Mrs Hendy's and today while she had ridden out; but at least her father was there in the house, useless and unobservant though he might be. Tomorrow there would be no one around at all, and Kirsty didn't like the thought of Dally coming round, taking stock of the horses and the layout of the stables and paddocks. She had intended to ask Lottie if she could come over; then she thought of Sheila, the owner of the brood mare who was due to foal. Fetching her address book, she dialled Sheila's number.

Yes, Sheila could come over; she'd been intending to, anyway. She could bring her sandwiches and keep an eye on things till Kirsty got back.

"You said you'd seen someone acting oddly up at Ravenswood?" Graham prompted. He opened the biscuit tin and sat down at the table, making a show of giving his attention to Kirsty. "Is it worth telling the police?"

"No." Kirsty reached across for her coffee mug and two biscuits. "He turned out to be the gardener. I'm going up for a bath."

Soaking herself under a mound of bubbles, Kirsty replayed her conversation with Dally. She could remember every detail: what he had said, how he had looked. At the time she had thought him weird, creepy; now, she couldn't really disagree with a single thing he had said. He had been criticizing the kind of overbearing horsey person she disliked and tried not to be: the person who used a horse as a status symbol, a winning machine. The Mrs Lucketts; Alison, forever battling with O'Leary to get him to arch his neck properly, using a whole armoury of bits and gadgets; the confident, loud-voiced people at shows. It all detracted from the horseness of horses. Their energy, their instinct and pure spirit, should be admired for themselves, not curbed and controlled. That was what Dally had been expressing. Not really, as she had thought at the time, some grudging class resentment, or hostility towards posh blonde women.

Kirsty's skin winced as she remembered the superior feeling she had allowed herself that afternoon, looking down her nose at Dally from Leo's saddle – yes, snootily – then making a great show of riding away, demonstrating her skill and flair. *Look at me, riding a class horse. Sitting prettily in my expensive saddle.* I belong to the club, and you don't. Dally was right – if Leo allowed her to sit on his back, to control and guide him, it was because of his generosity of spirit, nothing to do with her ability as a rider.

She ran more hot water and lay back, closing her eyes. She could only see Dally's face: his bony face, with its brooding expression, that should have been ugly; his deep-set, shadowed eyes that followed her everywhere.

CHAPTER 7

"Now Kirsty," Ursula said, when the waitress brought coffee, "it's time you made proper plans. Did some serious thinking."

"I *do* think. Quite seriously, a lot of the time. What else is there to do but think?" Kirsty took a chocolate mint and ate it, then rolled the foil wrapper into a tube. Phil, her mother's boyfriend, was affecting disinterest in this part of the conversation, sitting back in his chair and gazing absently around the restaurant. Quite right, too, Kirsty thought. It was nothing to do with him. Nothing much to do with Mum, either, since she'd decided to clear off to London.

It wasn't the local pub, after all – Ursula, of course, had made a booking, not leaving anything to chance. "There's this charming little place I've seen reviewed, beside the river at Bridford – I've been wanting an excuse to go there." Kirsty's objections about not wanting to spend long away from the yard were dismissed, and she was conveyed some twenty miles in the back of Phil's car. It was a four-door, to her relief. Nothing would have persuaded her to get into the back of a two-door. The restaurant was airy, conservatory-style, with glass-topped tables and lots of green plants, not at all oppressive. So far, so good. Kirsty enjoyed the freedom of choosing and eating something she hadn't shopped for and cooked herself – the delicate sauces, flavour behind flavour, the leafy garnishes and the soft grainy bread, all arranged on white plates as if for an art exhibition. She saw her mother watching her carefully while they ate, waiting for the right moment to launch her Get-Kirsty-Organized campaign. And now here it was.

"You know what I mean," Ursula said. "It's time you made some plans for your future."

"Why can't I stay as I am?"

Ursula's smile tightened, showing her determination not to be betrayed into sharpness. "Darling, you know we agreed this was just a temporary measure, till you got over your illness."

Illness. That was what she called it. A way of making it temporary and curable; in the past. Kirsty twisted the mint wrapper into a ring, then slipped it on to her finger.

"But it's certainly not too early to be making plans for September," Ursula went on. "Looking around. Going to open days. Making applications."

"What sort of course are you thinking of doing, Kirsty?" Phil asked.

Kirsty looked at him. "I'm not."

She saw her mother and Phil exchange glances; then Ursula said, "I can't understand why you're not bored out of your head stuck at home, tied to those horses, mucking out stables day after day, then skivvying indoors for Graham—"

"I don't see how it's any worse than what you do – choosing wallpaper for rich people in Putney," Kirsty said.

Ursula ignored that. "I mean, darling, what sort of social life do you have? I imagine you hardly see anyone, tucked away down there. You don't even see Ross any more, do you?"

"No," Kirsty said.

"Her boyfriend," Ursula explained to Phil.

"Ex-boyfriend," Kirsty corrected.

"Oh, I see." Phil nodded sympathetically. "No one new on the scene, then?"

Kirsty looked at his crisp shirt, bright blue with darker blue stripes, worn with a navy and white tie and a suit. He looked like a stockbroker. Why would anyone wear a business suit to go out for lunch? No one else in the restaurant was dressed like that. Ursula, too, was turned out as for a formal meeting, in cream linen. Kirsty, who had made quite an effort – putting on a little make-up, wearing a skirt for the first time in months, even wiping her shoes with damp kitchen towel – felt like a scruff.

"It's a shame about Ross." Her mother refilled all three coffee cups, and passed cream. "Such a nice boy, I thought."

Kirsty thought of Ross's bedroom, the rumpled cave of the duvet, clothes scattered on the floor. Her first time. Ross, lying back on the pillow, spent and triumphant. Her hands trembling as she pulled on her clothes, ears tuned for the sound of his parents' car in the driveway. Outside, her bike, her way home to completeness and separateness. It had been her last time, as well as her first.

"There'll be others, don't worry," Phil said jovially. He half-winked at Kirsty.

"I wasn't," she retorted. She picked up her spoon and turned it over. "Actually there *is* someone new."

Her mother inclined towards her. "A new boyfriend? Who's this?"

"I haven't known him long," Kirsty said. "His name's Dally and he's a gardener."

"Sounds like something out of D. H. Lawrence," Phil said. Kirsty had no idea what he meant. Ursula gave him a withering glance.

"A gardener – you mean a horticultural student?"

"Yes, that's right."

"Where's he training?" Ursula pursued.

"Oh, some college near Warwick. I can't remember the name."

"So how did you meet him?"

"In the village. He was on a placement locally. Doing a garden landscaping project."

"Well, how interesting. Garden design is quite the thing, nowadays. Why ever didn't you mention him, Kirsty? You'd have been quite welcome to bring him along."

Kirsty took a mouthful of coffee, almost spluttering at the thought of Dally sitting sullenly at the table with his torn jacket and unwashed hair, communicating in grunts.

"Anyway, I'm pleased to hear you're getting out some-times," her mother continued, "but let's not get sidetracked. Seriously, Kirsty, you're not telling me you're quite happy to carry on as a dogsbody? Most girls your age would be looking forward to earning real money, getting a car, getting some independence. And for that you need qualifications. Why don't you look out for a good business studies course? I can understand you not wanting to go back to school, after your year off, but there are plenty of sixth-form colleges around. You could even come and live with us if you wanted, and go to college in Putney. You'd still be able to see this boyfriend at weekends."

Phil looked wary, and Kirsty wondered if this were the first he'd heard of that idea. She thought about winding him up with an enthusiastic acceptance, but said instead, "When Jay comes back, things will really get going. With the horses. He wants to expand, he's got all sorts of plans. I can work with him properly then, and Dad can pay someone else to be housekeeper."

"Darling, has it not occurred to you that he might not come back?"

Kirsty stared. "What do you mean?"

"It strikes me as highly likely that he'll stay on in the States," Ursula said, in an infuriating breaking-it-gently tone. "Haven't you thought of that?"

"Of course he won't! The whole point of training with someone as famous as Matt McPherson is to help him build up a reputation when he gets back. He's going to take problem horses for schooling. You know!"

"And he can't do that in Connecticut? It hasn't struck you that he might be offered a job over there? Or that he might decide to settle with Emma, even get married?"

"He's coming back," Kirsty said flatly. "His horse is here. He wouldn't leave Leo."

"I'm glad to see you've got a clear sense of Jay's priorities," Ursula said. "Just bear in mind what I've said, that's all. I'd hate you to be disappointed. I mean, when did Jay ever make a plan and stick to it? You know what he's like." She said to Phil, "One wild idea after another, that's my son. When he was seventeen it was going to be a rock band; next, he was going to work in advertising. Then he got himself this horse and decided to be an Olympic gold-medallist – that's till the horse went lame. Then he met gorgeous Emma and off he went to the States. Impulsive, never sticks at anything. Somehow he always manages to land on his feet."

Phil raised an eyebrow. "Interesting life, though."

"You could say that. I just don't want Kirsty to be left picking up the pieces."

Kirsty put down her coffee cup; it clattered against the saucer. "You don't know what you're talking about!" Heads turned at nearby tables. "Can't you hear how you're contradicting yourself! He can't stick at anything, you say, but all the same you think he'll settle down cosily and get married –"

"There are temptations out there, that's all I'm saying," her mother said mildly. "A far more glamorous lifestyle, with Emma into the bargain – is he really going to leave all that behind, just to come home to the middle of nowhere, with those tumbledown stables and a few nondescript nags?"

" 'Scuse me."

Kirsty pushed back her chair and blundered to the Ladies', pushing past two chattering young women into a cubicle. She didn't need the loo; she stood leaning against the partition, an unwilling listener to the conversation of the other two. "I mean, give me a break, I told him – I've just about had it up to here, I said, and if you expect me to put up with any more of this. . ." from one, an accompanying murmur of "Mm, mm, right," from the other. She waited for the creak and swing back of the outer door, and the voice fading: "So I said to him, right? I'm going in there tomorrow and putting a deposit down, and if you don't like it you can just –"

The door clunked shut. Kirsty emerged. Now that the cloakroom was empty, the decor encouraged lingering – there was a cane armchair, a big oval mirror above sinks with marble splashbacks, boxes of pastel tissues. Kirsty took out her hair-brush and looked at the frail, startled girl in the mirror. A demure figure in a neat T-shirt and cardigan, with staring dark eyes. That's me, Kirsty thought, with a sense of surprise. That's all I am. That's what people see when they look at me: someone totally insignificant. She moved closer.

The scented air of the cloakroom thickened, clogging her lungs; her ears buzzed. The eyes stared back, mesmerizing her. It was her middle-of-the-night face, the face that didn't quite seem to be hers, that seemed animated by some other intelligence. The mouth would open and speak to her and tell her to do something mad, evil. To hurt someone.

The door opened and someone came in; Kirsty swung round. A kind-faced woman smiled at her and approached the mirror, smoothing back sleek hair, feeling in her bag for a lipstick. Kirsty looked down. Finding the brush still in her hand, she went through the motions of tidying her hair. She fumbled the brush back into her shoulder bag, then walked out of the cloakroom, past a blur of faces and greenery and reflected light on glass tables; on through swing doors and out to a riverside terrace.

She felt different outside, soothed by the sunlight, the weeping willows, the ripple of water. The terrace was set with picnic tables, but it was too early in the year for eating outside. One couple sat huddled in their coats, facing the river. They weren't speaking to each other, but they both smiled as she passed as if including her in their pretence that it was summer; Kirsty saw the jaunty tilt of a cocktail umbrella in the woman's glass. She walked to the end of the terrace, where she sat on the edge of the cold concrete with her legs dangling.

She thought of the lake at Ravenswood, the sweep of lawn, the grass-scented air, cool with birdsong. The fact of its existence, private and inviolate, was reassuring. If she didn't have to be here, she could be there. It would wait for her.

Below her feet, weeds trailed in the current like hair. She thought again of Ophelia in the painting, her pale drowned face. A moorhen bobbed along the shallows opposite, behind trailing fronds of willow, newly in leaf. There was a grass meadow crossed by a trodden path, then hedgerows and more trees blueing to hazy distance. Jay couldn't want to leave all this, Kirsty thought: however beautiful Connecticut is, it can't be more beautiful than England in late April. It was cold enough for her to wish she had her coat, but nice sitting here, with the clunk of crockery from inside and the murmur of voices.

Court shoes clopped along the paving, then stopped beside her. Kirsty squinted up. Ursula's expression was exasperated, on the edge of real annoyance.

"Come on, Kirsty. This is a bit melodramatic. You can't keep running away from things, you know."

"I'm not running away. I'm still here."

"Can't you see you're making Phil feel awkward? It was hard for him to make time to come today – he's got an important sales conference on Monday and work to do when he gets back –"

"Didn't ask him to come, did I?"

Ursula's chin tilted. "Please don't be difficult. I hardly see you anyway and apparently it's too much trouble to tear yourself away from the dung heap for a few hours. As for this in-your-face rudeness, as they seem to call it these days – it may be trendy but it's not pleasant. Not pleasant at all."

"All right. Sorry." Kirsty stood up slowly. "Are we going home now?"

"Phil's just settling up. And if you could remember to *thank* him for buying you lunch –"

"Yeah, I will."

"And Kirsty." Ursula lowered her voice and touched Kirsty's arm. "You are feeling better, now, aren't you? You still look a bit pale to me. I worry about you being anaemic. You don't think you ought to go to the doctor again?"

"There's nothing the matter with me." Kirsty picked at the strap of her shoulder bag.

"Are you absolutely sure? I mean, you'd have to come out in purple blotches or have fainting fits before *Graham* would notice anything amiss. How do you two get on together? I'd have thought you'd be at each other's throats by now."

"No, it's fine. We get on, Dad and I. It works out well."

Ursula looked sceptical. "Just make sure he doesn't take you for granted. You really ought to have a proper arrangement. A day off each week, if not more – a complete break now and then. Between the two of them, him and Jay, they'll have you running yourself ragged."

Kirsty turned away and gazed at the river. "I'm not going over all that *again*."

"You really ought to have a better colour," Ursula persisted, "being outside in the fresh air so much. Are your periods all right?"

Kirsty flicked an embarrassed glance at the couple at the picnic table; her mother didn't realize how her voice carried. "*Yes*, Mum. For God's sake! I'm fine, I've told you. Can we change the subject now? Let's go and find Phil."

All the way home, sitting in the leather-smelling rear of Phil's car, she held in her mind the vision of the unpeopled garden at Ravenswood: the sweep of velvet grass, the quiet expanse of water. It was like repeating a mantra, keeping the world at a safe distance.

CHAPTER 8

"Everything's fine," Sheila reported, back at Bramblings. She had taken up residence in the tack room, sitting in the one ancient chair, wrapped up in a scarf and anorak and reading *Cosmopolitan*. She was the least cosmopolitan person Kirsty could imagine – thirty-something, staid and stocky, always dressed in cord jeans, an ancient sweater and Clark's lace-ups. A transistor radio and an empty lunch-box rested on a pile of rugs.

"Isn't anyone else here?" Kirsty asked.

"Nope, only Alison – she's out riding. The Nellies have been and gone," Sheila said, "and as for my old lady, you'd think having a foal was the last thing on her mind." She put down her folded magazine on the rugs. Kirsty glanced at the feature she had been reading: *Sexual Politics for the New Millennium*.

"Thanks, Sheila, for waiting. Sorry I was so long."

Sheila shook her head. "No problem. It's been quite nice, really. I've made myself at home. D'you want a hand with anything? Morag turned Patches out, down in the bottom field with Leo, after she'd ridden him—" She clapped a hand to her mouth. "I nearly forgot! Someone called Danny came round looking for you."

"Danny? I don't know any – *oh*!" Kirsty felt the rush of blood to her face. "You mean Dally? Tall, skinny?"

"Yes, that's him."

"What did he want?"

"He didn't say. Just asked for you."

"Then went away again?"

Sheila nodded, putting her lunch box and radio into a shopping bag. "I don't know how long he'd been here, 'cos I'd been down at the schooling field helping the Nellies to put up some jumps. He was looking at Dorcas when I came back up." Sheila gave Kirsty an arch look. "Who is he? Boyfriend?"

"God, no. He's Mrs Hendy's gardener, round at Ravenswood – you know the big house? I can't imagine what he wanted." In spite of her revised opinion, Kirsty didn't like the idea of Dally being in the yard. Looking at the horses. Looking at a brood mare, vulnerable and unattended in her stable. . .

She thanked Sheila again and went down to the field to bring Leo in. The bottom field was at the end of a dipping track, out of view from the yard; Kirsty stood by the gateway, calling to Leo, who was grazing with Patches and the two fillies on the far side of the field. Anyone could be lurking down here, she thought. There was a dilapidated barn, thick hedgerow – plenty of cover for anyone wanting to hide. The field was lush and green, the horses grazing companionably in the afternoon sunshine – an idyllic picture, but someone was threatening to intrude. Someone was putting thoughts into her head that she didn't want there.

She took Leo back to his stable and groomed him, thought about riding and decided against it. There was still nearly an hour before she would need to start feeding. Back at the house, there was no sign of her father; she didn't expect him for hours yet. At least there was no need to cook tonight – they could make do with a sandwich, if Clare hadn't already fed him.

Dad and Clare, she thought, Mum and Phil; Jay and Emma. All these pairings-off. Why do people have to go away? If Dad decides to move in with Clare, then what?

Then, of course, Jay could come back here with Emma. That would make sense. The house was big enough for three of them. For more than three, if Jay and Emma had children. Thinking fondly of her future as an auntie, Kirsty went back to the yard for her bike and cycled to Ravenswood.

She rode round the track past the house and leaned her bike against the stable wall. Dally wasn't there. Caught between relief and disappointment, she spent longer than necessary grooming Prince, giving time for Dally to turn up; when he didn't, she looked for him by the toolshed and the hay-barn and even in the loft above the harness-room. There were no tools left in view in the garden: no wheelbarrow or rake or heap of prunings. Perhaps he had the afternoon off and had gone home. Or maybe he was in the house, having one of his cosy chats with Mrs Bishop. Kirsty wondered whether to make some excuse to go into the kitchen, thought better of it and cycled home.

By six o'clock, when she had finished work and went indoors, there was still no sign of her father. Hungry cats waited by their empty bowls; Moth made a pointed remark. Kirsty reached for a tin of cat food, thinking about tea and toast. Then the phone rang.

"Kirsty, love?" It was her father. "I've had a bit too much to drink, and Clare thinks it would be best if I stayed here overnight. You don't mind, do you?"

"No," Kirsty lied.

"How did it go? The lunch?" His words were leaning into each other, propping each other up.

"Fine, thanks."

"She didn't try to give you a makeover? Turn you into a sleek city girl?"

"No, we had a good time. They took me to a restaurant on the river at Bridford. It was really nice."

"Oh." Graham sounded mildly offended. "Look, I've got to go. I'll see you in the morning, then, around breakfast time? You've got Clare's number if you need anything. Oh, and Clare says hello."

"Yeah. Bye then."

Kirsty replaced the handset and stood frowning at the kitchen calendar, thinking uneasily about the drinking. She noticed something she'd forgotten – *Dad at Fulwell Manor* was written right across the dates for next Saturday and Sunday, in her own writing. Her father occasionally spent weekends tutoring courses for would-be writers, at a residential centre in Dorset. It was the first one since Jay had left, but there would be others. She would have to get used to being alone.

Saturday night. She remembered Tat, and the party at Ollie's, and her lies about Adam. She would have to invent something if Tat phoned tomorrow. She fed the cats, made tea and toast for herself, had a shower and half-heartedly watched some TV, flicking through the local paper.

There it was, leaping from the page: *Horse injured in knife attack*. Not much detail; the article concluded: *Police are linking this incident with similar attacks in neighbouring counties.*

She folded the newspaper. It had got into the house now, the thing she was trying to ignore. It had got into her head, and wouldn't be pushed away.

The cats were usually shut in the kitchen at night, but she let them come up to her room, for company. Wanting the dangerous hours of the night to be over, she went to bed early. Her routines were well-practised; she turned on her radio, hummed to the music, flicked through an old magazine, tried to keep her mind on normal, everyday things. The purr of cats reassured her as she turned off her bedside lamp, the rasp of Moth's tongue on fur as he washed himself.

She must have slept, but woke abruptly, much later. No nightmare: she had been woken by the insistent silence of a house with no one else in it.

Only a quarter-past four. She needed more sleep.

Insomnia was like toothache, prodding her to turn every few moments in an effort to arrange herself more comfortably. No use. Some while later she was still staring into the dark, wide awake. She got out of bed, put on socks and a dressing-gown and went into her father's study. He had made a perfunctory effort at tidying up before he left: there was no sign of *The Damage Done*, no scummy coffee-cups or used ashtrays. Kirsty drew the curtains to avoid seeing her reflection looking in from the blackness outside.

She turned on the computer and dialled up the internet connection, waiting for the modem to go through its series of bouncing clicks, then logged on to e-mail. *Collecting mail . . . Downloading 1 of 2.* Jay's name, as she had hoped, and *A Quick One*; then something from her father's agent. Kirsty clicked, and read:

Hi, Mouse! Thanks for yours. In a hurry, so just to say that's great about Leo. Remember he hates tractors if you ride out on the road. I'm glad everything's going so well. Let me know about the foal, make sure you call the vet if anything looks dodgy. And tell Mrs Nellie she's a stupid old bat. It's fantastic riding up in the Berkshire Mountains and the Appalachian Trail, you'd love it. E. and I went to Boston on our day off. Say hi to Dad.

Cheers! J.

78

He didn't say why he was in such a hurry, Kirsty thought. She read her father's message too, in case it was something exciting he'd want to know about as soon as he came home, but all it said was:

I spoke to Ed yesterday as arranged, but it was disappointing news, I'm afraid. They really don't feel they can take any more from you at present as sales have been so low. I'll try Celia at BH then get back to you.

Oh.

Kirsty didn't know exactly what that was about, but she did know that bad news from publisher or agent could throw her father into a slough of self-doubt and despondency that might last for days. He wouldn't be pleased to see that she'd already downloaded and opened it, either. She disconnected, then began typing a reply to Jay off-line. The whirring of the computer masked night-time sounds; first one cat, then another came in and settled, Nutmeg washing herself by Kirsty's feet, Moth sitting blinking on a pile of papers.

When she had finished her long, chatty message, logged on again to send it and inevitably been tempted into a little aimless net-surfing, she pulled back the curtains. The sky was already lightening; with the computer's whirr silenced, the air outside was full of birdsong. It was nearly half-past five, not worth going back to bed now.

She went down to the kitchen and made herself some Dad-style strong filter coffee. Outside, the sky was soft and rainwashed, dawn colours giving way to blue; hesitant early sunlight touched the tops of the poplars, making them look like paintbrushes tipped with fresh russety green. Into Kirsty's mind slipped the picture she carried with her of the garden at Ravenswood, the lawn spread out for blackbirds and thrushes, and the quiet lake. It would be beautiful now, in the secrecy of before-daytime.

Carried by her impulse, she washed and dressed quickly, fed the cats, then went outside for her bike. The hedges that bordered the lane to the village, black, thorny and impenetrable in winter, were now a paint-chart of freshest green and pinky browns, dotted with the delicate white of blackthorn flowers. Kirsty's tyres whizzed through the village street, where a cat blinked at her from the Post Office doorway. Being up and out before everyone else was like discovering a pleasant secret. How oddly time behaved, she thought. At night it stretched itself out like black elastic; now, in the sun-dappled early morning, each moment was a moment gained, a gift for her alone. Yesterday's cold breeze and overnight rain had worn themselves out, and the morning tasted of summer to come.

Ravenswood was asleep. The sound of tyres crunching on gravel seemed to bounce between the yew hedge and the stone frontage of the house, immensely loud. Kirsty dismounted and wheeled her bike along the grass edging. The lawns had been mown over the weekend, all of them, and the edges neatly trimmed. A huge job for one person, Kirsty thought, even on one of those sit-on mowers.

Prince wasn't looking out of his stable. Had someone taken him away? Fear clotted Kirsty's chest. She dropped her bike and ran to look over the half-door. He was lying down, legs folded under him, looking oddly small for such a big horse. Mildly surprised, he raised his head from dozing and his nostrils fluttered a greeting. Kirsty smiled, the peace of the morning resettling around her: the sunshine almost warm on her back, a pigeon cooing somewhere, the harsher caw of a rook.

"You stay in bed a bit longer," she told Prince. She righted her bike and parked it properly against the harness-room wall.

Walking across the lawn felt like walking into a dream. The garden had a separate existence now, inside her head. She could summon it whenever she wanted. In the dream version, the lawn was as remote and distant as a classical painting; in real life, it soaked her shoes and clad them in filaments of cut grass. The house receded as she walked slowly past the cedar with its umbrella of darkness, over the shoulder of ground towards the lake. The water shone coldly, reflecting sky and willows.

Something was splashing down there. At first she thought of moorhens or coots; then, when it was more insistent, looked for a swimming dog or maybe a fox in pursuit of waterfowl. Then she saw a bobbing head: sleek and dark, like a seal's, and pale arms thrusting forward.

A person. A someone. Swimming in Mrs Hendy's lake. At six o'clock in the morning.

She stood, caught between envy and fear. The swimmer hadn't seen her; he made a burst of fast crawl towards the deeper water in the middle of the lake, then rolled over lazily on to his back and blew out a water-spout. This was *her* place; Kirsty thought. She wanted it to herself. Who else had the right to be here?

Dally. Only Dally. It must be. Kirsty wondered why she felt so relieved. He wallowed and floated, enjoying the water, quite unaware that he was being watched. Should she call out? It seemed unfair to watch without him knowing; yet she was reluctant to interrupt. Silently, she moved towards the shelter of the weeping willow. Under its trailing canopy he had left a pile of clothes and a horse blanket.

Then Dally rolled over again, turned and looked in her direction. He stopped swimming and stared, ducked right under the water, then surfaced and stared again. He swam towards her, very slowly; then, reaching the shallows, he stood and waded out of the water. He looked like some mythical figure rising naked out of the dawn lake, streaming water. Kirsty's eyes were drawn to his ribby chest, his narrow hips, his penis in a nest of dark hair. He pushed his wet fringe out of his eyes and smiled, quite unselfconscious, as if it were perfectly normal to be naked in front of her.

"Hi. You're early." He picked up the horse blanket and started rubbing himself with it.

"I couldn't sleep. Weren't you cold?"

"Only at first. It's great. You should go in too."

Perhaps he seriously expected her to strip off all her clothes and plunge in.

"You're mad!"

"If you want," he said, quite seriously. He stopped rubbing. "For a minute just then I thought you were someone else."

Kirsty laughed. "Mrs Hendy? I bet she doesn't get up this early. She doesn't know what she's missing." Her voice sounded loud in the still air; how far did it carry? More quietly, she said, "It must be deeper than it looks, in there." Now that he had waded out, the lake surface had closed again, mirroring sky, giving away none of its secrets.

"In the middle it is. You have to be careful of weeds at the far end."

Dally continued to dry himself, shivering a little. He made no effort to hide under the blanket, rubbing himself vigorously. He wasn't flaunting his body either, as some boys might have done; he was simply getting on with it, as if she weren't there. He seemed completely indifferent as to whether she looked at him or not. She looked. He was unexpectedly graceful for someone so tall and thin, not bony and awkward as she would have thought; he was all long arms, long thighs, long sweep of curving spine as he bent to rub his legs. Kirsty thought: I'm not afraid of him, not now. She didn't really know why not. She leaned against the sinewy trunk of the willow, suppressing a giggle at the thought of Mrs Hendy looking out of her bedroom window and seeing what she would see.

"Aren't there tadpoles and things in there?" she asked, wondering if he smelled of pond. "Snails and frogs and wriggling things?"

"I hope so. That's what lakes are for, for things to live in them. I'd go to the swimming pool if I wanted chlorine. I like this better."

"Your feet are all muddy," she pointed out.

Dally looked down at his pale feet, his long bony toes. "I'll wash them again in a minute."

He flung down the blanket and pulled on pants and jeans. Kirsty wondered why he hadn't brought a towel. She recognized the horse blanket, with its striped edging – it came from the harness-room, and was one of the clean ones stored in the trunk.

"Dally?" she said.

"Yeah?" He was rubbing his hair, his voice muffled by blanket.

"You don't go home at night, do you?" she ventured. "You stay here all the time. You live here."

He lowered the blanket and looked at her. His hair was a wild tangle round his face.

"Yeah, that's right."

"Where do you –? I mean, not in the house?"

He laughed. "Course not. Can you imagine me in there like Lord Snooty, in some great ancestral bedroom with a four-poster bed? Having dinner with old Mrs H at the end of one of those great long tables?"

"Then where?"

"Gardener's cottage. Behind the rose garden. Haven't you seen it? I'll show you if you want."

"You mean, it's – official? It goes with the job?"

He looked at her. "No. No one knows. You don't have to tell anyone."

"You're a squatter?"

Dally smiled, buttoning his shirt. "S'pose so. Only to be a squatter, people have to know, don't they? Someone has to mind you being there."

"Wouldn't Mrs Hendy *let* you live there, if you asked?"

"Dunno. It's easier like this." Dally picked a strand of dark-green weed from his wrist. "No one bothers me."

Where do you really live? What about your family? Have you got a family? All Kirsty's questions baulked voiceless on her lips.

"You can be my first guest," Dally said. "I've never invited anyone round before. Come and have breakfast."

Breakfast – Kirsty imagined toast and coffee, a table in a sunlit kitchen, a window looking on to a vegetable patch all neatly dug over and staked for runner beans. Dally waggled a foot in the water, then sat on the blanket to dry it. Kirsty felt unaccountably touched by the care he took over each foot in turn, drying between his toes, giving his full attention. He pulled on socks and boots, then stood up, folding the blanket.

"Come on then. Breakfast *chez moi*. You might change your mind when you see. It's a bit primitive."

"Primitive?"

"No running water, no electricity. That sort of thing."

They walked across the lawn towards the walled garden. A brown blackbird shouldered its way across the lawn in a series of muscular hops, watching them alertly; then it found a worm, jerking and stretching it out of the ground.

"She's got chicks to feed," Dally said. "There's a nest by the cottage. They'll be leaving it soon."

He seemed more talkative than usual, more relaxed. He led the way through the gate and past the topiary peacock, along a grass path between symmetrical, formal beds, all planted with twiggy rose-bushes. There was a classical statue at the far end, in a wall alcove – a woman with trailing hair and Grecian robes, in a sorrowful pose with one hand held to her face. Behind the wall were high trees: the wood that gave Ravenswood its name. There was another gate at the far end, which grated as Dally opened it.

Kirsty stepped out of the garden.

It was quite different out here, on the other side of the wall. There was a muddy cart-track between the wall and the edge of the wood. The wood was full of birdsong; between slender trunks Kirsty saw the tight purplish stems of bluebells and the freshness of dog's mercury. Facing the gate was the gardener's cottage, brick-built and actually quite large, with a lean-to shed. It had a paling fence enclosing a front garden completely overgrown with thistles and nettles.

Dally draped his damp blanket over the paling fence to dry. Then he unlocked the front door. Kirsty thought: no one knows where I am. She followed him inside.

CHAPTER 9

"Primitive, like I said." Dally stood by the doorway, waiting for Kirsty's reaction.

Inside, the cottage was bare. The front door led straight into the main room, with narrow wooden stairs leading up. The floor was of wooden boards, the windows uncurtained. The room smelled of woodsmoke and dust. In one corner Dally had set up camp – there were horse-blankets on the floor, an unrolled sleeping-bag, a Calor-Gas camping stove. Beside the fireplace was a heap of chopped wood; charcoal crumbled in the grate from a recent fire. Several crates were stacked against the wall, next to a large rucksack, and a carrier-bag filled with something soft. Kirsty saw candles – a half-burned-down one stuck in a flower-pot, and a packet of new ones; there was no electricity, she remembered. A stable broom was propped by the fireplace, and the floor had been swept clean. It was cold in here, out of the sunlight.

"Is this it?" Kirsty said awkwardly. "Your worldly possessions?"

Dally stood throwing his key from one hand to the other. "It's amazing how little you need when you don't have much," he said. "You ought to try. Makes life so simple."

Kirsty couldn't see where the breakfast was going to come from. Perhaps he had used the promise of breakfast to lure her in. Tendrils of fear uncurled in her stomach. Dally might lock the door behind him; he was bigger and undoubtedly stronger than she was. How long would it take before anyone looked for her in this abandoned cottage? Dad wasn't even at home to report her missing.

"What do you *do* all the time?" She tried to keep her voice calm and level.

Dally shrugged. "Sleep. Read. Think."

"Have you been here all through the winter?"

"No. I'd have died of exposure. I moved in a week ago, ten days. I forget." To her relief, he put the key in his jeans pocket and moved away from the door. Now she could run away if she wanted to, but curiosity made her stay. "What about you?" he asked, in his abrupt way.

"What about me what?"

"Coming to look after the horse." Dally pulled out a crate, stood another on top of it, then went to another and took out a bag of bread rolls, a carton of milk and a tub of margarine.

"Oh. Months. Since last autumn, when my brother went away. He did it, before."

Dally appeared not to hear, rummaging in another crate. "There's marmalade, somewhere. Only one knife, though. We'll have to share. Tea or coffee?"

"Coffee, please," Kirsty said. She laughed; it came out edged with hysteria.

"Have a seat. Pull up a crate." He gestured to the two stacked ones, which were evidently going to serve as a table. Then he poured water from a bottle into a small saucepan, found matches and lit the camping stove. Its blue flame gave out a feeble warmth. Kirsty held out her hands to it. Through an open doorway, she could see a kitchen – ancient and utilitarian, with a big square sink and draining board, and all the plumbing visible. Not much use if the water was turned off. There were two saucers by the kitchen door – one containing remnants of meat, the other milk.

"Whose is that?" Kirsty asked.

Dally turned. "Freda's. My cat. Well, not really my cat. She comes from the farm on the other side of the wood. She turns up here quite often."

"Did you give her that name, Freda?"

Dally nodded. "Wrap yourself up in a blanket if you're cold. I could light a fire, only it's not really worth it. I'll be going out after this."

Kirsty felt reassured by the fact that Dally had a cat. Someone who liked cats and had named one Freda seemed unlikely to lure people into deserted buildings in order to mutilate or kill them. "What time do you start work?" she asked.

"When it feels like the right time. I haven't got a watch."

"So you never know what the time is?" Kirsty, who was always looking at her watch, calculating whether she could fit in this or that, couldn't imagine being free from time's constant demands.

Dally brought out one chipped mug and one glass, and spooned out coffee. "Don't want to know. Don't need to. When it gets light it's morning, and when it gets dark it's night. That's all you need. Sorry, I can't do toast, but these bread rolls probably aren't too stale. I get them from the village shop. If I'd known you were coming I'd have bought fresh ones yesterday."

Kirsty giggled. Dally looked at her quizzically. "What's funny?"

"You are," she said. "So *polite*. Like we're having a posh meal up at the house, with a linen tablecloth and silver knives and forks."

Dally found a bag of sugar and a spoon, digging in the bottom for the remnants. "Do you take it?"

"No, thanks. Don't you usually have breakfast in the house?"

"Sometimes. When Mrs B takes pity on me."

"But she doesn't know? About this?"

Dally shook his head. "No, she just thinks I need feeding up. I've always got room for two breakfasts. Three, if they were going."

"How did you get to be a gardener? Do you know all about gardening?"

Dally shook his head. "Not much. I just tidy up and cut the grass and mend things, a bit of painting, odd jobs, whatever I'm told to do. There's an old bloke who comes round once a week – he used to be head gardener here about a hundred years ago. He tells me what to do and I do it."

He brought out a white plate, rubbed it on his shirt-sleeve, and arranged the bread rolls on it; he put the plate on the crate-table, together with the margarine tub and the pot of marmalade.

"Why did you come round yesterday?" Kirsty said. It came out as an accusation. "To the yard. When I was out."

Dally looked at her, offering no explanation. He was so peculiar, she thought, never responding the way she expected. His silence forced her to ask again, "What did you want?"

"Where were you?" he asked bluntly.

How did he make her feel that she was the one who needed an excuse? She gave it. "My mum came to take me out to lunch."

"She doesn't live with you?"

"No, she left last year." She heard the catch in her voice. "She . . . got bored with Dad, I suppose. With all of us. She lives in London now, with her gruesome boyfriend. He came yesterday as well. I didn't want to go."

"Why did you, then?"

He looked at her, waiting for an answer. She didn't give one. What business was it of his?

"So who lives in your house?" he asked.

"Just me and my Dad. But my Dad wasn't there last night. He stayed with Clare, his girlfriend."

"You were all on your own?"

"Yes. And again next weekend." Before the words were out of her mouth, Kirsty thought: *Why am I telling him this? I must be mad. I know nothing about him.*

Dally picked up a bread roll and broke it in two, the crust cracking. He said fiercely, "He shouldn't leave you like that. You shouldn't be there on your own. Have some bread."

Kirsty took a roll and reached for the margarine. Dally passed her the knife, then busied himself with the coffee, pouring bubbling water from the saucepan, adding milk, stirring it with a fork. "Here." He passed her the mug, keeping the glass for himself. "You can warm your hands on that. I'll come and stay, if you want."

"Stay?"

He stirred sugar into his glass. "Next weekend. So you're not on your own. Just at night, I mean."

Kirsty clasped her mug, silenced by the outrageousness of the idea. Bring him home? Let him spend the night in the house? He must be joking.

"Is that why you couldn't sleep?" he said. "'Cos you were on your own?"

"Yes." She looked at him to see if he thought she was a wimp. "I have dreams. Bad dreams. I get frightened." The words just came out. "Sometimes I think I'm going mad. I'm scared of my own thoughts."

Dally nodded slowly, as if he knew already. He broke off another piece of bread.

"Why did you come round?" she pursued.

"The police came here," Dally said. "I didn't know if you knew."

She stared at him. "About?"

"About someone attacking horses. Some madman." He tore at the crusty bread with his teeth.

Kirsty felt herself flushing. She couldn't look at him.

"Who'd *do* something like that?" she asked. "Who'd want to hurt a horse?"

"Dunno. There are all sorts of weirdos about. People who hurt animals just 'cos they can, for kicks." Dally took another bite, then said with his mouth full, "If he comes round here, hurts Prince, or any of yours, I'll kill him."

"How d'you know it's a he?"

"It'd have to be, wouldn't it? Women don't do things like that. It's some pervy bloke."

"But it might be *they*, not he."

Dally gave her a sharp look. "Anyway, you knew about it?"

"Yes, Lottie told me," Kirsty said. "You know, my friend, the one you call posh. And the police phoned us."

"But your Dad still leaves you on your own?" Dally said. "What's wrong with him?"

"I don't know. He – he doesn't take much notice of things. He doesn't think things are important, I mean not the things I think are important, or that most people would. He's a writer, he's too wrapped up in his work."

"That's an excuse?" Dally huffed.

"He needs to concentrate," Kirsty explained. "He can't be bothered with everyday ordinary things."

"Why don't you tell him you don't like being on your own?"

"Because." Kirsty took a gulp of coffee. "I don't talk to him about things like that. I just get on with it."

But she was talking now. Telling Dally things she hadn't told Tat, or Jay. It gave her an odd sense of recklessness. He sat on the crate, leaning forward with hunched shoulders, listening.

"Who *do* you talk to?" he said.

"No one. I'm used to it. Who do you?"

He gave a sudden wolfish grin. "Talk to? Freda. The blackbird. The air. I'm used to it."

"Haven't you got friends?"

"Friends, yeah." He shrugged. "They're there when I want them. I don't, at the moment. I'm taking time out."

"Out from what?"

"From living in the normal world, I s'pose. I like it better here."

"Won't you go back?"

"When I want. Not yet."

He poured more water into the saucepan and re-lit the camping stove. Kirsty ate her roll, giving him quick, covert glances. She studied his face, his nose with the prominent bony bridge, his thin cheeks and heavy eyebrows, and his mouth that had a characteristic down-turn but could break so unexpectedly into a smile that was more fierce than amused. His eyes were so deep-set that it was hard to tell what colour they were – grey, she had thought when he looked straight at her, but maybe grey-blue or grey-green. She thought: he's ugly, he must be, and yet there was something in his face that was not ugly at all, something more appealing than bland good looks. Presumably he must shave sometimes, she thought, noticing the glint of stubble on his chin and upper lip: how odd to bother, living here like this without water or electricity. Why not just let it grow?

"Mirror," she said suddenly. "Have you got a mirror?"

He paused, crouching, about to top up his glass of coffee. "No. What do you want one for?"

"I just thought, you haven't got one," Kirsty said. "I'd like that, I think. No watch and no mirror."

"Here, give me your mug," Dally said. "Like I said, it's amazing what you can do without, once you start. If I wanted a mirror, there's the window. Or the lake. Want more coffee?"

Kirsty thought: there's a story, isn't there, a Greek legend or something, about someone who gazed into a lake at his own reflection? She took the refilled mug. Warmer now from the coffee, she began to feel that this was almost normal: sitting here, talking, unhurried. Drowsiness fogged her brain, and she remembered that she had hardly slept; it wasn't surprising that she was tired. After this, she'd do Prince's stable, then go home and see if Dad was back. She glanced at her watch. When she'd finished the feeding and the stables, there was Nellie to groom and the tack to do; it was still an ordinary day, even if it had had an extraordinary beginning. Later, if there was time, she might ride out on Leo. Perhaps even sleep this afternoon, if it was quiet.

She finished her coffee quickly and stood up. "I'd better go and do Prince. It's Sunday, and all the livery owners come. Thanks for the breakfast."

"OK."

Dally didn't look up, or go with her to the door.

"See you later," she called from the door.

He didn't answer.

"Yes, we heard it on local radio at lunchtime," Mrs Luckett said. "Two horses, retired hunters, out in a field near Letchford, both with stab wounds in the neck. Terrible."

"When did it happen?" Kirsty asked flatly. Letchford was only six miles away.

"Some time yesterday, I suppose. They didn't say much. Gemma's awfully upset, aren't you, love?"

Gemma, leading Nellie out of the stable, turned down her mouth and eyes to show how upset she was.

"What happened to the horses?" Kirsty asked.

"Both had to have stitches. One was injured worse than the other. Kirsty, to tell you the truth," Mrs Luckett confided, "I'm beginning to think we might have to move to Wolverton after all. It's nothing personal – we know you do your best, but you're so vulnerable out here, aren't you?

Anyone could come snooping round. At Wolverton they've got an alarm system and a guard dog. Gemma'd never get over it if anything happened to Petronella."

"As long as you can afford it," Kirsty said waspishly. Tiredness was beginning to make her irritable. She looked at the pony's sleek coat, at the saddle and bridle she cleaned every single day, and thought of the Nellies' weekly cheque – but doubled at least – going to Wolverton Equitation Centre. Please, no. She didn't want to have to explain that to Jay.

"Perhaps the police'll catch someone this time," Mrs Luckett said.

The telephone extension bell shrilled. Kirsty excused herself and went into the tack room to pick up.

"It's me," said Lottie's tearful voice. "Have you heard? It's awful."

"Oh Lottie, what?" Kirsty's instant thought was that Mrs Nellie had got it wrong, and that it was Lottie's Puzzle that had been stabbed.

"Another horse attack. Oh, Kirsty, I can't bear to have Puzzle out of my sight! If anything happened to him I'd just die!"

Kirsty thought of Leo out in the bottom field, and Dorcas the brood mare, heavy in foal. What could she do? Wild ideas surged into her mind – a Securicor man with a dog; complicated alarm systems; herself corralling all the horses together and keeping guard over them through the night, armed and ready for combat.

"Do you want to come round?" Lottie said tearfully.

Kirsty looked at her watch. Two o'clock. She had done all her yard jobs. "Yes. About an hour, OK? I'll ride round on Leo."

She rang off. There were plenty of people about: the Nellies, who would fuss round for a good two hours yet, Alison, schooling O'Leary in the field. Looking out of the tack-room door, Kirsty saw Sheila's red Golf pulling into the yard. Safety in numbers.

Yesterday, she thought. Saturday. Someone went into a field with a knife and deliberately hurt two horses.

She replayed her conversation with Dally, heard herself asking: "Who'd do something like that? Who'd want to hurt a horse?" Dally: "There are all sorts of weirdos about. People who hurt animals just 'cos they can, for kicks."

It wasn't him. It couldn't be. But if it was, she had just told him that she'd be alone here next weekend.

She lingered in the tack-room for a moment to straighten the dangling reins of Leo's bridle and pick up some scattered brushes, soothing herself with the warm leathery smells.

Her father had arrived back at lunchtime, when Kirsty was making herself a sandwich. He'd already had lunch, at Clare's. After a brief exchange – "Hi there, sorry I'm a bit late, everything OK?" "Yes, thanks, had a good time?" – he went straight upstairs and Kirsty back to the yard. Now, she

99

marched indoors and straight up to his study. He was only reading the Sunday papers, not working.

"You can't go off again and leave me here on my own!" she burst out. "There's some maniac around, attacking horses. Something happened yesterday."

"Oh God, another one," Graham said wearily. "Have the police phoned again?"

"No, but it was on the radio, and Lottie told me. Honestly, Dad, anything might happen! I can't seriously believe you're going away for the whole of next weekend?"

"Am I? Where?" Graham shoved a heap of papers aside, found his diary and turned the pages. "God. Fulwell Manor. *Structuring the Novel.* Just as well you reminded me – it had gone clean out of my head."

"So you're still going, then?" Kirsty leaned against the door frame, exasperated. "Didn't you hear what I just said?"

"I'll have to ring Clare – she was going to get theatre tickets." Graham frowned at his diary, then looked up at Kirsty. "I can't let them down at Fulwell, no, not at such short notice – they'd never ask me again, and the money's quite good."

"Oh well, if there's *money* involved," Kirsty retorted.

But they needed money. She knew that. Graham's earnings from writing were unpredictable, and never enormous. He did odd bits of reviewing and journalism to supplement the money from his books, and the weekend writing courses paid quite well. He grumbled about them – "all those no-hopers with their tedious manuscripts" – but always said yes when he was asked. The cheques from Fulwell Manor were just as necessary to the household as the horses' livery fees. Of course he couldn't back out, not now. But then what? Kirsty couldn't face the prospect of two more sleepless nights, listening to every creak and gurgle of the empty house.

Graham tapped a pen against the cover of his diary. "No, you're right. You shouldn't be here alone. Tell you what – I'll ask Ursula to come and stay."

"No! You know Mum – she'll nose round everywhere, carry out a full house inspection!"

"Clare, then? Shall I ask Clare to come over?"

Kirsty thought about it. She had only met Clare on three or four occasions, and quite liked her – she wasn't bossy or fault-finding, like Mum. There was a sort of quietly-spoken firmness about Clare. She'd need firmness, Kirsty thought, to put up with Dad. All the same, Kirsty didn't want Clare to think she needed a child-minder.

"I'll ask Tat," she said. "She can come and stay."

CHAPTER 10

"Oh, but I can't," Tatjana said, on the phone. "I'm off to Berlin tomorrow."

"Berlin?"

"Told you, didn't I? History trip. I'll be away till Tuesday next week."

"Yes, I remember," said Kirsty, who didn't.

"So anyway, how did it go?"

"How did what go?"

"Kirsty!" Tat reproved. "The weekend! Adam! Mysterious hunky Adam!"

"Oh." Kirsty summoned enthusiasm into her voice. "Yes, great! We had a really good time."

Tat huffed. "Is that all you're going to tell me? So when are you seeing him again? When do I get to meet him?"

"Actually," Kirsty improvised, "it's a real shame you're going away at the weekend, 'cos he's coming over. That's why I wanted you to come. Still, some other time. . ."

"So your Dad knows now, then?"

"Oh yes. He's fine about it. So's Clare. They're both really pleased."

"I definitely want to meet this guy when I get back from

Berlin," Tat said. "Don't think you can keep him all to yourself."

When Kirsty rang off, she thought that she really ought to keep notes of the lies she told. There were too many possibilities for catching herself out. Or perhaps she could stop doing it. She had told nothing but the truth to Dally – too much of the truth. Not all of it, but not a single lie, either. That must prove it could be done. As it was, she would have to invent something for Tatjana about Adam going back to Warwick; maybe she would say it was all over, that Adam had gone off her or met someone else. If she tried to keep up this pretence, Tat would soon be demanding full details of whether she'd had sex with Adam yet – if not, why not, and if so, what it was like. Kirsty had formed a strong picture of Adam: she saw him as fair-haired, muscular and sporty, extrovert, uncomplicated – the complete opposite of Dally, in fact. It came as a surprise to remember that this version was purely fictional. A pity. It would have been useful to have someone like Adam around.

Plan B then, since Tat couldn't come over. Kirsty fetched Leo in from the field, brushed him over and saddled him, and rode over to Lottie's.

The Holcroft place was something between farm and smallholding. Lottie's father, ten years older than Kirsty's, had once rented several more acres and managed a dairy herd, but since his stroke it was as much as he could do to look after a small flock of sheep, a few young beef cattle and a vegetable garden. It was occupational therapy, according to Lottie. He spent most of his time tending the vegetables, patiently weeding and composting and staking. The cattle were turned out now, the yard empty apart from a few hens. The eggs and the vegetables and the livestock brought in a bit of money, but not much, and the Holcrofts lived in fear of the rent going up. Puzzle was a luxury they could barely afford. Kirsty's father made hay for the winter and Puzzle was a robust pony who lived mainly on grass, but nothing could reduce the vet's or blacksmith's bills. Lottie needed her fantasy young farmer for practical as well as romantic reasons.

Kirsty put Leo in Puzzle's stable, Puzzle having been turned out with the sheep and lambs.

"We haven't told Dad about this latest attack," Lottie said, in the kitchen. "It gets him agitated, and there's nothing he can do about it."

The Holcrofts' two dogs, pale golden Labradors, lay snoring in a basket. Lottie's mum was cooking something complicated involving many different spices and three kinds of citrus peel; she was carefully zesting limes with a special gadget, while two lemons and two oranges queued up to be zested next. She was, Lottie said, the world's best cook and the world's worst clearer-up – every meal she prepared required dozens of bowls, plates and utensils, covering every available space. Kirsty liked the Holcrofts' kitchen, which was even more messy and disorganized than the one at

Bramblings. A battered teddy-bear sat in the vegetable rack and children's paintings were pinned to a board; the twins, Henry and Harriet, could be heard scampering from room to room upstairs.

"I'm sure they're trampolining on the beds again," Mrs Holcroft said. "I've *told* them not to," and she wiped her hands on her apron and went up to see. Lottie made tea, and she and Kirsty perched on stools. The air was full of the sharp tang of lime.

"There's fruit cake," Lottie's mum said, returning. "Can you find it, Lottie? In that tin with the parrots on it. Yes, it's awfully worrying, this business. We've got the dogs, but I'm not sure how effective they'd be, dozy old things."

Kirsty explained about her father's commitment for next weekend, and asked whether Lottie could come and stay. "You could bring Puzzle, if you didn't want to leave him here. He can stay in one of the spare stables, or go out in the field if you'd rather."

"That'd be OK, Mum, wouldn't it?" Lottie asked.

"Yes, I suppose so," Lottie's mum said doubtfully.

Then the back door opened and Lottie's father came in. He stood on the doormat, smiling vaguely at Kirsty.

"It's Kirsty, Dad," Lottie said.

"Take your boots off, love," Lottie's mum said. "There's tea and fruit cake. With cherries in – you like that."

Kirsty watched as slowly, obediently, he took off his muddy wellingtons, toe to heel, and stood them side by side on the mat, aligning them with immense care, like a child. He wore navy-blue overalls which he had fastened with the buttons done up wrongly, so that the fabric bunched at his chest and the collar stuck up oddly. She had known him before he was like this; he was like a blurred, out-of-focus version of his former self. He said something that only Lottie's mother seemed to understand, and sat on a stool, looking straight at Kirsty with his puzzled, amiable expression. Self-consciously she said, "It's a lovely day today, isn't it?" and he nodded slow agreement. He was a big man, which made his childishness especially poignant. What must it be like, Kirsty wondered, to be divided from your real self by a trick of the brain, a small seizure that threw the whole system? Did he know? Was the real man still there inside, endlessly frustrated by the gap between thought and action, the failure of words to come when they were needed? Lottie had cut his slice of fruit cake into small pieces but still he fumbled with it, dropping crumbs to the floor. One of the dogs, Juno, wagged her tail lazily, not bothered enough to heave herself out of the basket.

It was impossible now to say more about the horse attacks. Lottie went over to him and did his buttons up properly; then they chatted about the weather and the lambs and how the grass was growing, and watched Lottie's mum squeezing juice from her scalped fruits and stirring it into the pudding mixture. When Kirsty heard strident neighing from the yard, she got up to go. It wasn't impossible, after all, that someone could be lurking even now, in daylight, while she and the Holcrofts sat unaware in the kitchen. But Leo was unharmed, just bored; scrape marks showed where he had been pawing the stable floor, and his hay was untouched. He pranced and sidled as Kirsty led him out.

"He looks great," said Lottie, who had come out so that they could talk about the weekend. She gave Kirsty the necessary leg-up. "Jay's going to be so pleased with all the work you've done."

Kirsty hoped so. They made their arrangements for Friday, and she walked Leo home along the lanes, pretending he was her own horse. The day had kept its morning promise. From Leo's height, she looked across green verges, green hedgerows, to a landscape whose softness was splashed with the sudden citrus yellow of oilseed rape. Its cloying sweetness filled her nostrils, carried on the faint breeze. Leo walked alertly, keen for home and his evening feed. She looked down at the arch of his neck and his fine black mane that she kept neat and trimmed, and thought of a hand clasping a knife, holding it poised, thrusting –

Dally, swimming in the lake. His head bobbing like a seal's, his clothes in a pile on the bank. Supposing he was swimming to clean himself up, to wash away blood? He was up so early because he'd been –

No. No. That really was ridiculous. Dally wasn't like that. He hated the thought of anyone harming horses; he'd said so.

Said so. Kirsty thought of all the things she said that weren't true. Was Dally as accomplished a liar? She pushed Leo into a trot and hurried him along the lane home.

"Kirsty, come and have a look at this," her father called when she went indoors.

She went up to his study. He had an e-mail message on the screen, from Jay. Standing behind his chair, Kirsty read:

Dear Dad and Mouse,

Didn't want to tell you this till I'd made all the arrangements, but I'm coming home for a week! Flight booked, arriving Heathrow next Monday morning, 10.15. Any chance of you picking me up? If you've got a lodger in my room, please kick him out! Looking forward to seeing you both, also horses, cats etc. J.

"Oh, Dad!" Overwhelmed, Kirsty threw her arms round him. He laughed, clasping both her arms; she rested her chin on the top of his head and read the message three more times to make sure she'd understood it properly.

"Knew you'd be pleased."

"*Pleased!* It's great! Fantastic!"

"You need something to cheer you up," Graham said, screwing his head round to look at her. "You've been looking a bit down, lately."

"No! Just a bit tired. But this is – oh, a fantastic surprise!" Kirsty disentangled herself, unable to stand still.

"Pity it's not a couple of days earlier," he said. "That would have solved our weekend problem."

"No, it's OK, Lottie's coming!" Kirsty felt light-headed, all her worries dissolving. "Did you know about this? Jay hasn't phoned or anything?"

"No! First I knew was this message. I've only just logged on."

"I wonder why he's coming?"

"You can get cheap flights nowadays. Perhaps he's saved up some free time. Or he's homesick."

"I must get his room ready, and tidy up, and make a shopping list –"

"You don't have to start right this minute," her father teased.

And groom Leo every day this week, Kirsty thought, and carry on exercising him, and get some nice food in the freezer. "Do you think Emma's coming, too?"

"I should think he would have said. I'll ask when I mail him back. But it won't make much difference, will it? She'd sleep in his room."

Actually, Kirsty thought, it would make a lot of difference. She wanted Jay to herself. She wanted him to inspect the yard and praise her for her work, for keeping everything going. She wanted to ride out with him – she'd have to demote herself to Nellie or Patches – and stand in the sunshine looking at Dorcas' foal, which would surely be born by then. All she wanted was for it to be perfectly ordinary, as if he'd never gone away.

"I need to start a list," she said. Graham fished a piece of paper out of his waste-paper bin and passed her a pen: she pushed papers aside to clear desk space and wrote: *Blacksmith, feed order, tidy schooling field, sort rugs, mend gate.* Everything had to be in perfect order, a testimony to her competence.

"I might invite Clare over one evening," Graham remarked. He clicked the mouse, and a reply screen came up, with Jay's original message marked by chevrons. "And Adam, while he's still at home." He began typing a reply. **Mouse is leaping about like a two-year-old filly**, Kirsty read over his shoulder.

Over the next few days, Kirsty worked tirelessly. She rode Leo every day and groomed him thoroughly, trimming his mane, tail and heels. He was shedding his winter coat and beginning to look as sleek and pampered as a racehorse. She cleaned his tack, brushed his rugs and even whitewashed the inside of his stable. Lottie, as excited as Kirsty, came round to help; together they tidied the schooling paddock and shovelled dung into a barrow, and tried to make the makeshift collection of poles and oil drums look more like proper jumps. Kirsty dusted and hoovered Jay's room and made up the bed. She cleared up the worst of the clutter from downstairs, and made an ever-lengthening shopping list. Her father would do the main supermarket run on Friday, before he left, with another trip on Monday for the fresh stuff.

The twice-daily trips to Ravenswood became a nuisance, difficult to fit into the flurry of activity. The weather had turned cold again, cold and showery, with overnight frosts, so that the sunlit morning by the lake seemed impossible; even Dally wouldn't be stupid enough to swim, these chilly mornings. Blackthorn winter, Lottie called it; the late frosts coming with the white sprinkling of blackthorn flowers. It was one of her father's country sayings. Kirsty wondered if he still knew what it meant, in the slow churning of his thoughts.

She saw Dally a few times, but he seemed not to want to talk much; he didn't hang around the yard, or invite her to the cottage again. She wondered whether he regretted letting her know his secret, just as she regretted telling him some of hers. Occasionally Kirsty thought of phoning the police about him; or of simply telling Mrs Hendy that he was living in her gardener's cottage. She did neither. Dally was peculiar, she decided, but not dangerous. Having no shortage of peculiarities herself, she felt in no position to judge.

On Wednesday, the blacksmith came to fit new shoes for Leo and O'Leary and to trim feet for a couple of others. There were two of them: Eddie the blacksmith, and his apprentice, Richard, known as the blacksmith's boy, though he was nineteen and over six foot. Richard, who only came when there were several horses to do, grinned at Kirsty as she led out O'Leary.

"Going to hold on to him for me? Looks a bit troublesome, that one."

O'Leary was perfectly well-mannered and could easily have been tied to a wall-ring. Kirsty knew that Richard wanted to chat to her while he worked. He was a handsome boy, and knew it: fair-haired and blue-eyed, tanned from the hours he spent outside. He stooped with his back to her, lifting O'Leary's foreleg. In spite of the cold wind he wore a thin shirt with sleeves rolled up over muscular forearms.

"You coming to the point-to-point on Sunday week?" he asked.

"What point-to-point?"

"Come on, you can't have missed the boards by the main road! Over at Hurst Farm, other side of Newington. Give yourself a day off and I'll buy you a drink."

Eddie was heating a shoe at the mobile forge, holding it with tongs until it glowed red, then banging it into shape. "You want to watch him, Kirsty," he warned. "He's like this with all the girls."

"No, I'm not!" protested Richard, who probably was. "I mean it!" he said to Kirsty. "See you at the beer tent before the first race and you can buy me a drink."

"Oh, so I can buy *you* a drink now?" Kirsty said. "Thanks."

"That's right, you be careful," said Eddie. He held the hot shoe against Leo's hoof, checking the fit. "Thought we might see you in the Ladies' race. This nag of yours here can go a bit, can't he?"

"Leo isn't fit," Kirsty said. "Maybe next year, when Jay's back, he might enter him. Actually, Jay's going to be here next weekend. Yes, perhaps we'll come." It would be a good afternoon out, watching the races with Jay for company, his expert eye assessing the horses and their chances. She could cope with that. A crowd of people in the open air was less threatening than a quarter the number in a stuffy room.

"Oh well, if you've got big brother as chaperon –" Richard said, affecting deep disappointment. "Still, some other time, eh? When big bro's not around."

Kirsty stood by O'Leary's head, holding the headcollar rope and stroking his soft whiskery muzzle, watching the blacksmiths work. The air smelled of heat and metal and singed hoof, overlaying the warm smell of the horses. By the paddock fence that faced the yard Dorcas was steadily grazing, calm and big-bellied with the foal inside her. The feed-bins were full, the tack-room tidied, the yard swept. Kirsty looked at the reward for her work, at the groomed and well-shod horses; contentment warmed her. Jay was coming home, and it would soon be summer. This is mine, she thought: mine and Jay's. She wanted nothing else.

CHAPTER 11

"Bye then, Mouse," Kirsty's father said, jingling his car keys. "You've got my phone number, haven't you? What time's Lottie coming round?"

"This evening some time. Bye, then. Hope your no-hopers aren't too hopeless!"

"Oh, they will be. I don't know though – if there're any good ones, I get neurotic in case they're better than me! I can't win. See you, then. Back around four on Sunday, I should think, unless the roads are snarled up."

Kirsty watched the car until it disappeared round the bend in the lane. Loneliness settled round her like a cloak. She went back indoors, into the empty house, and cleared up the lunch things, determined to stick to her new rule of tidiness until Jay came. Moth sat on the window-sill, looking at her with squinty amber eyes. "It's all right for you, Mothy," she told him. "*You* don't care, do you? As long as you get your Whiskas twice a day." Then she heard her own voice in the high-ceilinged echoiness of the kitchen, and thought: listen to me, talking quite seriously to a cat. It would be different next week – Jay in the house would be more than just one extra person. It would be like having a proper family.

The phone rang in the yard when she was measuring out the evening feeds. She ran to answer it, carrying Leo's bowl of crushed barley and horse-nuts.

"Kirsty, I'm awfully sorry," Lottie said. "The thing is, Dad's not well, at least not actually ill, but having one of his panicky turns."

"So you're not coming after all?" Kirsty said bleakly. She saw the night hours stretching in front of her, an uncrossable abyss.

"I'm awfully sorry," Lottie said again. "The thing is, Dad's going to get himself in a right state, I mean if I'm not around. He gets like that. We can't explain to him. I really am awfully sorry –"

"Stop saying that! OK, you can't come. It's not your fault."

" – but Mum said, d'you want to come and stay here instead? We can put the camp bed in my room."

Leo was banging on the door, impatient for his feed. Kirsty thought about it. Obstinacy made her answer, "No, I can't stay away overnight. I don't want to leave Dorcas, when she's so near foaling. What if it went wrong?"

"You could get up really early –"

"No, I'll stay. I'll be fine. I sleep like a log, honestly, and I don't mind being in the house on my own. Dad thought I might like the company, that's all. Some other time, then."

"I'm awfu— I mean, it seems awful to let you down at such short notice."

"You can't help it. Never mind. I hope your Dad gets better."

Lottie promised to come round in the morning, and rang off. Kirsty went into Leo's stable, tipped the feed into the manger and stood leaning against his neck while he ate greedily, stamping his hoof as if she were an irritating fly.

"Oh, Leo! What am I going to do?"

Only three days and Jay would be here. Only two nights to get through on her own. Only. She finished her yard jobs and went to look at Dorcas, who was pulling at her hay-net.

"Dorcas? What about this foal, then? You can't hang on to it for ever!"

Sheila had told Kirsty what to look out for – any restlessness, pawing or getting up and down – but the bay mare looked perfectly composed, eyeing Kirsty calmly as her jaws worked rhythmically on the hay. Kirsty had made up a deep straw bed, banked at the sides, and had already brought in the special heat lamp which was suspended from the ceiling. If it stayed as cold as this, the foal would need the extra warmth.

"I'll come and see you again later," Kirsty told her. If the birth really had seemed imminent, she would have phoned Sheila, who wanted to be present. But Dorcas looked as if the thought of foaling had never entered her head. She ought to know, having had three foals already. Kirsty went indoors and fed the cats, and got a pie out of the freezer for her own supper, heating some beans to have with it. She could never be bothered much about food when she was on her own. When she looked out of the front window she saw that the Richmonds' cars were both parked outside; they were home for the weekend. That meant there was someone on hand, if she should need help. When she went to bed she would think of them on the other side of the dividing wall, so that the house wouldn't feel so empty.

She made herself a mug of tea and tried to watch some Friday night TV, but couldn't settle. After flicking from channel to channel, finding nothing to hold her attention, she went to the back door and pulled on her coat and boots, and went out to the yard.

All was quiet. Kirsty usually enjoyed this last tour, when all the work was done, nothing much to do except straighten a slipping rug or refill a water-bucket. She went round the yard, looking over each stable door in turn. Patches was lying down with all four legs neatly folded under him, like a china ornament horse. Dorcas was dozing on her feet, blinking in the electric light; no foal tonight, Kirsty decided. She heard the scampering of mice somewhere, and the scrape of hooves on the floor from Nellie's box as the pony scrambled to her feet and came to look over her door. Leo was alert, nickering a greeting, pushing his nose into Kirsty's hand as she went to his box. It was still twilight, not really dark; down towards the fields she could see the silhouettes of trees against a grey sky ragged with cloud, and a sliver of moon.

She decided to walk down to the bottom field, where the fillies were turned out. They were two-year-old Anglo-Arabs, bred by a local rider who hadn't got room for them at her own yard. They would stay turned out until they were old enough to be broken for riding, in about eighteen months. Useful, Jay said – bringing in the small amount he charged for grass livery, but needing no attention other than a quick daily checking-over. Kirsty, always afraid they'd escape or get themselves tangled up in wire, checked them at least twice a day; this would be her third visit.

Away from the lights of the yard, her eyes adjusted to the dimness and she could see quite clearly. Oddly, she felt less afraid, out here with her feet brushing through long grass, than she did in the house. The fading light had a peculiar intensity, so that the hedges and gateways seemed to be pushing themselves towards her. The cow parsley beside the track was coming into flower, holding its pale umbrella heads above the grasses. At the bottom gate, Kirsty looked across the sloping ground of the field; the fillies, a bay and a dark chestnut, were grazing by the far hedge, side by side, quite safe. No one was about. She leaned on the gate, breathing the evening air that smelled of grass and soil and the faint sweetness of blossom. There was a kind of triumph in standing here alone, keeping guard over the young horses, as if she had chased her fear away by confronting it. Out here in the twilight, knowing the land, knowing every gateway and clump of trees and dip in the ground, she was stalker rather than stalked.

In no hurry to go back indoors, she climbed the gate and walked slowly up the field edge. Fresh leaves of hawthorn and wild cherry touched her face, and her feet moved silently in the close-nibbled grass. Not much grazing left here, she thought; tomorrow, she'd move the horses to the smaller barn field, and leave this one to rest. She wanted Jay to know she was managing the grassland properly. She'd have to ask Lottie to help her, because one of the fillies could be difficult; they ought to be groomed and handled more, taught to lead properly. . .

She climbed the fence at the end of the field where it dipped by the water-trough and crossed the smaller paddock towards the buildings.

There was someone in the yard.

Her heart lurched. The lights were still on and she could see the silhouette of head and shoulders, leaning over Dorcas's half-door. Dorcas, vulnerable and slow, wouldn't strike out and defend herself with hooves and teeth, as Leo surely would if attacked. Kirsty, in an agony of indecision – Dash for the house? Run to protect Dorcas? – held her breath. Then the figure turned away from the door and became recognizable, with bony profile, slim shoulders, deep-shadowed eyes.

Dally. Of course.

Kirsty let herself out of the gate and walked towards him. The latch made a clicking sound as it closed.

"Hello," Dally said. "Wondered where you were."

"I've been at the bottom, checking the horses down there," Kirsty said, trying to keep her voice normal. There, she was doing it again – telling him that there were horses turned out in the field, well out of sight of the house. What was the matter with her?

"I've brought my stuff," Dally said, gesturing towards a rolled sleeping-bag on the ground. "I'll sleep in the tack-room if that's OK."

"Sleep?"

"Told you I was coming round. You haven't forgotten, have you?"

"You offered," Kirsty pointed out, "but we never said you actually *would* –"

"I never say things I don't mean," Dally said. For a second his voice was edged with anger. Then he added, more kindly, "I didn't mean to make you jump, just now."

"OK," Kirsty said flippantly. "But there's no need for you to stay here. I'll be fine."

"You won't," Dally said. "Your dad's away and you'll have nightmares or stay awake all night. I'm staying. You don't have to do anything. You can go indoors now and I'll sort myself out in the tack-room. I've got a book to read." He stooped to pick up his sleeping-bag.

"I don't see what it's got to do with you," Kirsty said.

"I'm your friend, aren't I?"

"Are you?"

At that moment Dorcas, interested by the voices, came to

the door and lifted her head over, nuzzling Dally's shoulder. He turned and raised a hand to her cheek, scratching gently; then he bent down and blew into her nostrils, each in turn. The mare breathed back at him, intrigued.

"She thinks you're another horse," Kirsty said. "You're good with horses, aren't you? How? Where did you learn?"

"I didn't learn. I just know," Dally said, stroking the mare's ears. Then he looked directly at Kirsty. "You think it's me doing the attacks, don't you? That's why you're scared of me. That's why you don't want to leave me here with the horses."

"No!" Kirsty said quickly. But there was something about Dally that compelled honesty. "Yes. Sometimes," she amended.

"So why haven't you phoned the police?"

"How do you know I haven't?"

"You haven't," Dally stated.

"No."

"Are you going to? You can, if you want. You can phone them now. You've got a phone down here, haven't you?"

"Is that what you want me to do?" she challenged.

"Not really, 'cos I'll get thrown out of the cottage. But go ahead."

Kirsty shivered and pulled up her coat collar. The lights of the yard threw everything beyond into blackness. Dorcas went back to her hay. One of the other horses let out a long, shuddering breath, and a hoof stamped.

"No," Kirsty said.

For a second, Dally seemed almost disappointed. Then he said quietly, "It's not me. I'd never hurt a horse. Any animal. I want to catch the pervert who's doing it, that's all."

Kirsty pulled her coat closer around her. "I'm going in now. I'm going to make some coffee. You can come, if you want."

"Do *you* want?" Dally said.

She nodded uncertainly. He dumped his bed-roll by Dorcas's stable and followed her up through the garden. She had left the kitchen lights on. Moth came from somewhere out of the shadows and ran in with them, then twined himself round Dally's legs, purring. Kirsty cleared various bits of clutter off the table, making space for Dally to sit down. She bustled about, filling the kettle, spooning coffee into mugs, very conscious of Dally's silence and her unaccustomed role as hostess.

"Are you hungry? Have you had anything to eat? I can make toast, if you like."

"Thanks."

Kirsty looked in the fridge. Some of the things in there were for Jay's visit, not to be touched, but she found a packet of bacon and some sausages.

"D'you want these? I've already had something, but I could do you a fry-up."

Dally looked at the packets in disdain. "No, thanks. I don't eat dead animals. Do you?"

"Do I eat meat? Yes, I do."

Some vegetarians she knew – Tatjana, for one – would have taken the chance to give a lecture on factory farming and moral responsibility, but Dally said no more. His silence seemed to say: *You eat animals and I don't, and you think* I'm *the person attacking them?* Moth had jumped up on to his lap and was trilling with pleasure at being stroked, butting his head against Dally's chin. Kirsty watched with surprise.

"He's usually nervous of strangers," she said.

Dally glanced up. "So are you."

"Yes, well –"

Kirsty wondered why Dally wasn't more resentful of her suspicion; he had a way of accepting whatever she told him without surprise or comment. She found tomatoes and baked beans to cook with the toast; she made the coffee and gave Dally his. He had taken a paperback book out of his pocket and was reading it, bending it back on itself in a way that made Kirsty wince. Her father would blow a fuse if anyone did that with one of his books.

"What're you reading?" she asked.

Dally held the book up to show her, and she saw that it *was* one of her father's. *Foxtail.* She saw the ruddy swirl of fox-brush across the cover, her father's well-known photograph on the back. She stared at Dally.

"Where'd you get that?" For a wild moment she thought he must have broken into her father's study and stolen it.

Then she noticed its plastic jacket and a red sticker on the spine.

"Library," Dally said.

"Did you know Graham Millen's my dad?"

"Why d'you think I got it out?"

"I didn't tell you his name. I didn't even tell you that he's a writer."

"Mrs Bishop told me. I asked her. I had to go to the launderette yesterday so I went to the library while I was waiting. They had two others on the computer but I only found this one. The woman there said, 'Oh, you're lucky to find one on the shelves. He's our local author, Graham Millen, did you know? Such wonderful evocative prose. We're all longing to see his next novel.'" Dally had put on a high, twittering voice. He added, as himself, "I think he's a shit, your dad."

"How can you?" Kirsty was fired into defensiveness. "You've never even seen him."

"I'm reading this, aren't I? This is him. All this *I'm-so-sensitive* stuff. All this '*sharp, uncanny insight into adolescent angst*'," he read from the cover. "Oh yeah? What does he know about it, if he clears off and leaves you on your own? What does he know about *you?*"

The tomatoes in the pan were beginning to brown. Kirsty picked up the wooden spatula and flipped them over. "He didn't mean to leave me on my own. Lottie was supposed to be coming, but then she couldn't, after all. Anyway, it's his work! He has to go. He has to make money."

Dally looked sceptical. "*Wants* to go. He can make money with his wonderful, evocative prose, can't he? From his desk at home. What's he writing now? Something else about adolescent traumas?"

Kirsty said nothing, concentrating on the cooking to avoid saying that yes, her father was a shit. She knew his two selves well enough, his literary persona and his private one. The food provided a distraction now that everything needed doing at once; the baked beans were spluttering, the tomatoes ready, the sliced bread popping out of the toaster. Dally turned another page, and said no more until Kirsty put his plate in front of him. Then he plonked the book face-down on the table.

"Got any brown sauce?" he asked.

She fetched it, and sat down opposite. He squeezed out a liberal dollop and began to eat fast; he always seemed ravenously hungry. In the time it took Kirsty to eat her one piece of buttered toast, he had cleared the whole plateful without stopping to say a word. It was as if she'd brought a half-starved dog into the kitchen to give it a good feed. She went to the larder and brought out a packet of chocolate digestives.

"What about your mum?" he asked abruptly, mopping up brown sauce with the last bit of crust.

"I told you. She left. They split up."

"No, I mean what's she like?"

Kirsty hesitated. "Very different from Dad. Bossy. Not in

a nasty way, just – I don't know – interfering. I mean she's ambitious, she wants everyone to be good at whatever they do, really good. That's why she got fed up with Dad, I suppose. It was all right at first, when he started to get published. But to Mum, he'd never be a real success unless he won the Booker prize or got a film deal or something. She couldn't understand why he wasn't pushier, why he just let things happen or not happen."

"You don't get on with her?"

"I don't know. I used to. I don't know how it all changed, really. I mean, I used to tell her things about school and friends, ask what she thought. And then when I got to thirteen or so, I stopped talking to her, and next time I wanted to, she wasn't there. It was like –"

Dally pushed his plate away and reached for a biscuit, looking at her expectantly.

"It was like being a mother was just one of the things she'd set herself to do," she went on. "You know – be the perfect mum, OK, done that, now I'll be an interior designer. That's what she does now." She felt her mouth twist with regret, remembering what it had been like here at first, coming home to find the kitchen table strewn with fabric swatches, the air smelling of fresh cotton, Mum busy and slightly dishevelled in jeans and a sweatshirt, with her hair escaping from a pony-tail. "She's busy, successful. She's got a new life and she can't see why we're still stuck in the old one, Dad and I."

"Why did you think it was your fault she cleared off?" Dally said, crunching, spilling crumbs on the table.

"Who said so? I didn't."

But a memory slid into Kirsty's mind, of lying awake, tears spilling from the corners of her eyes and wetting her hair against the pillow: *I'm not good enough for her, not clever enough, not pretty enough, not worth the effort. . .* She gulped at the dregs of her coffee. Silly. Stupid. Of course it wasn't her fault. It was Mum and Dad, their argument, their divorce. Loads of people had parents who'd split up.

"Anyone can be a parent," Dally said, "whether they're any good at it or not. Half of them shouldn't be allowed."

"What about yours?" She took the chance to steer the conversation away. "Have you got parents?"

Dally looked at her in amusement. "No. I came out from under a gooseberry bush."

"Seriously! Have yours thrown you out or something?"

"No." He said it on a rising note, like a question.

"Come on – I've told you about mine, but I don't really know anything about you. Where do you come from? Where do you live? Where did you go to school?"

"School?" Dally spoke with utter scorn. "What d'you want to know about that for?"

"Oh!" she huffed. "This isn't fair – you won't tell me anything! You know things about me, or you find them out, but you won't say anything about yourself!"

"I told you," Dally said, pushing his plate away, "I've left all that behind. Parents, school. None of it matters any more. What you see is what you get. And I don't know much about you, do I? I don't need to. I don't need to know what your favourite subject was at school or who your favourite group is or where you'd like to go on holiday. I know what I know. I know what it's like inside your head." He said it quite matter-of-factly.

"You think so, do you?" Kirsty was amused by his arrogance. "How?"

"Because I do. Right. I'm going to bed, now," Dally said, standing up. He took three more chocolate digestives from the packet. Kirsty thought of his bed-roll, left outside in the yard.

"You don't have to go out there. You can sleep on the sofa if you like," she offered.

Dally shook his head. "The whole point is for me to be out there. In case anything happens."

"Well – there's some horse-blankets down there. In a pile in the corner. A bit spidery, but –"

"I'm used to that. You do lock this door at night, don't you?"

"No, I leave it wide open, with a sign saying *Please come in.* What do you think, with prowlers about?"

He nodded. "See you in the morning, then."

Kirsty washed up, turned off the lights and went up to her room. From her window she could see nothing but the lane to the village, and the pale moon behind wisps of cloud.

Undressed, she crossed the landing to Jay's room and looked out towards the yard. Dally had turned the lights off, but she could see a crack of light from under the tack-room door. She pictured him stretched out in his sleeping-bag, on a pile of rugs, reading her father's novel. Back in her own room, she took her copy of *Foxtail* from the shelf, getting into bed with it. Dally had read about a quarter, she had seen from the way he bent the pages back; she opened her own copy at about the same place, imagined Dally reading her father's words, and wondered what he thought of them.

It would be cold out there. Dally was used to it, but all the same she felt that she should have been more hospitable, insisting that he stayed indoors. She was puzzled by his interest: in her father, his books, even – so he claimed – the inside of her head? Dally was weird, no doubt about it, but she no longer felt threatened by his weirdness. She thought: if I can't sleep, if I wake up in a panic at two in the morning, Dally will be there. With the cats settling around her, making soft purry sounds and trampling her duvet and catching it in their claws, she turned off her light.

CHAPTER 12

Kirsty woke with the early daylight, surprised to find that she had slept through the night without waking once. It was a quarter to six. The cats were still with her, stretching luxuriantly as she stirred. She reached up to part the curtains and look out of the window. It was a still, bright morning, the low sunlight touching the treetops along the lane into brilliant green and bronze, while the ground was in shadow.

She remembered Dally. She got out of bed and dressed quickly, and ran downstairs followed by cats. Outside the back door, the air was as fresh as cool water, promising warmth to come.

The tack-room door was wide open. He's gone, she thought; he's left me here on my own, after all. Then she saw him. He was inside Dorcas's stable, leaning against the half-door, with his back to it. As she approached, he turned and put a finger to his lips.

Kirsty crept up to the door and looked over; then she caught her breath. Dorcas was suckling a tiny chestnut foal which stood on splayed legs. Kirsty saw its short woolly tail waggling while it drank, and the damp curls of its coat. The mare turned her head to touch the foal with her nose, nudging it.

"Oh! When did she –"

"A few hours ago now. It all happened quickly once she started."

"Oh, and I missed it! Why didn't you call me?"

"Couldn't, could I? The door was locked," Dally pointed out.

"I don't believe it! After all this waiting."

Kirsty tried to remember all the things Jay had told her to check. Dally had already switched on the heat lamp, which was wired up to the tack-room; he had given Dorcas more hay, and the bedding was clean, with fresh straw spread. The foal's coat was dark chestnut in colour, dried from birth by the mare's licking. It was a colt, Kirsty could see.

"You've done everything right!" she told Dally in surprise.

He shrugged. "She didn't need any help. She knew what to do. Instinct. All I did was watch."

"And did he suckle all by himself?"

"I helped a bit. Showed him where to go."

The foal finished drinking and gave a spluttery sneeze, then turned uncertainly and raised his head to stare at them. He had a crooked white blaze down his face, from domed forehead to whiskered muzzle, and a short dark mane that curled up in tufts. He had a compact body in which the bone structure was prominent, and an alert little head.

"Oh, he's gorgeous!" Kirsty whispered. "I must phone

Sheila, she'll be so pleased! But I feel awful, leaving it all to you. I wonder if I ought to get the vet to come, just to check?"

Dally was watching the foal too, smiling. It wasn't his usual fierce grimace, but an open, unguarded smile that Kirsty hadn't seen before. It made him look far less formidable. "He's a strong, healthy foal," he said. "No need for the vet, is there?"

For the first time Kirsty noticed the wheelbarrow parked in the corner of the yard, loaded with soiled straw and the bloody mess of the afterbirth.

"Did you have to cut the cord?" she asked. Dally, astonishingly, seemed to have proved himself as a capable equine midwife.

"No, it broke by itself."

"There's some stuff in the tack-room. I've got to dress the stump, so it doesn't get infected. Isn't it amazing how quickly it's all happened? There was no sign last night, or if there was, I missed it. You're brilliant, doing everything right! How did you know what to do? Most people would have been hopeless!"

"It's only common sense." Dally let himself out of the stable and slid the door-bolt quietly. He yawned and rubbed his eyes, then looked at Kirsty blearily. "I'm going now, then. They'll be OK."

"Don't. Not now!" Kirsty pleaded. "I'm going indoors to make her a mash. You can crash out on the sofa, if you want. It's still early."

Kirsty didn't want to be alone – not through fear, but through a wish to continue sharing the mood of triumph with someone. With Dally. The spring sunshine, the successful birth of the foal, Jay arriving the day after tomorrow – she had so many reasons to be happy. Dally, drooping with weariness, followed her to the house. She showed him to the sofa; he took off his boots and stretched out, and was heavily asleep by the time she returned with a blanket from upstairs. She laid it carefully over him and stood for a moment looking down at his sleeping face. He looked younger, vulnerable, the harsh lines of his face smoothed out, his mouth slightly open.

What you see is what you get, he had said about himself, meaning straight, open, uncomplicated. But Dally was the last person the phrase could be applied to. What she saw was only what he chose to let her see.

Kirsty boiled a kettle for Dorcas's mash, then went back outside to feed all the horses, turn out Leo and O'Leary and do the mucking-out and yard jobs. When she had swept and tidied, and spent a few more minutes leaning over Dorcas's door to admire the foal, she went in to feed the cats and make breakfast. First, she went to see if Dally was awake, taking him a mug of tea. He was still sleeping, with Moth tucked in smug and squinting by his side, and Kirsty was about to tiptoe out again; then he groaned and stirred, opened his eyes and gazed at her unrecognizingly for a second. What had woken him? She had taken care not to make a sound; he must have felt her presence, sensed some change in the air.

"Oh – what. . ." He sat up, running a hand through his tousled hair. Moth jumped to the floor with a small protesting remark.

"I've brought you this." Kirsty proffered the tea. "But you can go back to sleep if you like."

"It's half-way through the morning," Dally said blearily.

"No, it's not even nine o'clock yet! If you're staying awake, I'll make you some breakfast."

"Thanks," Dally said. He looked at her, blinking. "Any chance of a shower? I could do with one."

"OK! I'll show you."

She took him up to the bathroom, showed him how to adjust the temperature and where the shampoo and shower gel was, and fetched him a clean towel. Downstairs, she sliced bread for toast and scrambled four eggs. She wasn't sure what Dally's policy on eggs was likely to be, so she fried some tomatoes just in case. He took a very long time in the shower; not surprisingly, Kirsty thought, if he usually had to boil up water on his camping stove, or else swim in the lake. Hot water must be an unbelievable luxury.

The cats. She'd forgotten to feed them. "Come on, Nutmeg! Moth! Breakfast!" she called, forking out Whiskas, shaking biscuits into a bowl. The cats rushed in and lined themselves up by their bowls in the way that always made

Kirsty think of cows in a milking parlour. She was pouring milk for them when Lottie's voice in the doorway made her jump, and slosh milk on the cats' mat.

"Kirsty! I've tied Puzzle to the gate and I just looked in and saw the foal! Isn't he gorgeous!"

"Oh – you're early!" Kirsty said, flustered.

Nutmeg obligingly lapped up the spilt milk. Lottie stood inside the door, flushed and excited.

"Yes, I thought I'd come round straight away. What time was the foal born? Did you stay up all night?"

Kirsty saw Lottie registering the bathroom sounds from above, the two plates set out to warm. A frown creased her forehead. "Oh – is your dad here after all?" she asked.

"No, it's Dally. You know." Kirsty waved a hand in the general direction of Ravenswood. "He stayed here last night. He's in the shower."

"*Kirsty!*" Lottie's mouth dropped open; her eyebrows shot up like opposing arrows.

Kirsty thought, not for the first time, how very different her two friends were. Tatjana would have responded with an amused lift of one eyebrow and a few pertinent questions; virginal Lottie was horrified.

"No! I don't mean – Lottie, he was great! He was the one who looked after Dorcas. I slept all through it. He did everything right."

"But you hardly *know* him! And you were the one who thought he was weird!"

Kirsty heard the shower click off overhead, and the thump of feet on the floor. Dally would be down in a minute.

"He is weird," she said. "But in a nice way. He came and stayed last night 'cos he knew I'd be scared on my own."

"Are you going *out* with him now?"

"No!" Kirsty was amused at the idea. "He isn't the sort of person you go out with." Where would you go, with Dally? To sit by the lake? Lean over the paddock fence?

"Then what?" Lottie pursued. "He seems quite at home here." She rolled her eyes towards the ceiling. "Does your dad know?"

"There's nothing *for* him to know! We just talked a bit, that's all." Kirsty couldn't tell Lottie about the cottage at Ravenswood, or about Dally swimming in the lake. "And then he slept in the tack-room."

"Really," Lottie said. "Actually I came to tell you that Dad's much better and it'll be OK for me to stay tonight. But maybe you don't want me to, now you've made more interesting arrangements."

"Lottie, don't be daft! Thanks! That's great!"

"But if *he'll* be here," Lottie said sniffily, "I needn't bother."

"Of course he won't! There won't be any need, if you're staying. D'you want some breakfast? There's plenty to go round."

"Had some, thanks. Anyway, I don't want to disturb your cosy twosome. I'll wait in the yard."

"No, don't! Please don't go all huffy. Have some tea, at

least. Oh – I haven't phoned Sheila! I need to ask if she wants the vet to come out. Can you stir the scrambled egg?"

Sheila, delighted with the news of the birth, wanted full details even though she was about to get in her car and come over. As Kirsty put the handset down, Dally came into the kitchen with wet hair slicked close against his head, and stared at Lottie as if she had no right to be here.

"Oh, Dally," Kirsty said awkwardly. "You've seen Lottie before, haven't you?"

"Yes. Hello," Lottie said, in a voice stiff with disapproval.

Dally said nothing. He gave one of his Neanderthal grunts and sat down at the table.

"Here, let me." Kirsty took the spatula from Lottie, gave the scrambled egg a final stir and started serving the food. "Pour the tea, can you? Lottie came to tell me that she can stay tonight after all," she told Dally.

She passed him his breakfast, remembering to put out the brown sauce. He started eating without a word of thanks. He hadn't put his shirt back on and was wearing a T-shirt whose days of being white were long past, and which showed his skinny arms. Lottie poured the tea and grudgingly put a mug on the table for Dally, who made no acknowledgement. She turned to Kirsty with a silent, reproachful glance.

"I'm going out," she said. "See you in the yard."

"Lottie, wait –" Kirsty said, but Lottie had closed the door firmly behind her. Kirsty brought her own plate to the table and sat opposite Dally. "Oh dear," she said. "Sorry.

Lottie got it all wrong – you know, with you being in the shower, and being here for breakfast –"

She had tried to sound jokey, but Dally showed no interest in what Lottie might have assumed. His face had assumed a distant, unapproachable expression; almost, Kirsty thought, he had turned back into the peculiar, taciturn stranger she had seen at first. She could hardly believe that he had talked to her last night, and smiled, and been as happy as a visiting uncle about the foal's birth. He finished his breakfast without looking at Kirsty; then, leaving his plate where it was, he pushed his chair back and stood up. "I'm late for work. I'll collect my stuff and go."

"Hang on! Will I – will I see you later?"

Dally stared at her blankly. "You'll be round to do Prince, won't you? Or do you want me to do him today?"

She was disappointed by his indifference. "If you could turn him out when you go back, I'll do the stable and everything this afternoon. Thanks. And thanks for coming last night. And for everything."

"OK," Dally said, and went.

Kirsty hadn't finished her own breakfast, but she didn't feel like it now. She scraped the leavings of scrambled egg into the cats' bowls and cleared up the kitchen, then went upstairs to the bathroom. Dally's black shirt was lying there on top of the Ali Baba washing basket. She picked it up, wondering whether he had forgotten it, or whether – from the way he had behaved in the kitchen just now – he expected it to be returned to him, washed and ironed. It was fine black cord; the label inside the collar was an exclusive and desirable one. Surprised, she fingered the fabric of the sleeve. How could Dally afford such an expensive shirt?

She cleaned her teeth and brushed her hair. Her face looked pale and anxious; her hair was a mess and needed washing, but there wasn't time now. She must have made a most unfavourable comparison to Lottie in the kitchen – all tumbling hair and flushed indignation. But, she thought, Dally didn't look twice at Lottie. It's me he's interested in. Not in the way Lottie thinks, and not necessarily all the time, but – he is.

What does he see? What *is* there to see?

Her eyes looked steadily back at her, like someone else's, providing no answer.

She walked down to the yard and into an altercation.

Alison, O'Leary's owner, was standing there with her horse all tacked up and ready to ride, venting her feelings on Lottie.

"Did you *hear* him? The way he spoke to me? Who is he, anyway?"

"I know, he's loopy, absolutely loopy –"

"What's the matter?" Kirsty looked from one to the other. O'Leary stood quietly, unperturbed – clearly, nothing had happened to upset *him*, to Kirsty's relief.

"That boy, whoever he is," Alison fired back. "That's what's the matter. Comes strolling into the yard as if he owns the place, then marches up to me and starts ranting about O'Leary's tack."

"His *tack*?"

"Yes! Like he's the world's leading expert or something. 'What d'you need all that for?' he went. 'If you were half a rider you wouldn't need gadgets.' Then he goes, 'What right have you got to force him to hold his head the way you want and hit him with whips?' Or something like that. You heard, didn't you?" Alison said to Lottie.

Lottie nodded. "Yes – 'He's a horse, why can't you just let him be a horse, instead of turning him into a circus animal?' That's what he said."

Kirsty looked to see precisely what O'Leary was wearing. Alison was always experimenting with different bits and martingales. Today, she was using a Pelham bit with a curb chain, and a running martingale.

"I said to him, 'I'd like to see *you* controlling him when he takes hold. Think you could do that with just a piece of string?' and he gives me this weird look and goes, 'That's what it's all about, isn't it? Control,' and he looks at me like I've crawled out from under a stone, and walks off. Honestly, he must be a complete nutter. You ought to be more careful who you have hanging round the place. Who is he, anyway?"

"Friend of Kirsty's," Lottie said. "He works at Mrs Hendy's."

"Your *friend*?"

"Yes, he is," Kirsty said, "and he's OK, really."

"Well, he doesn't look it to me!" Alison checked her horse's girths and tucked one of the bridle straps into its keeper. "You want to choose your friends more carefully, Kirsty. If he speaks to me like that again, there'll be trouble, right? And I don't want him anywhere near O'Leary."

"I'll be friends with who I like!" Kirsty retaliated.

Alison gave her a sceptical look. "Fine. Let's hope you don't mind losing customers, then." She pulled the near-side stirrup down its leather and mounted. O'Leary, who had been standing obediently while they talked, was now expected to jump smartly to attention as Alison's black-booted legs clamped against his sides. Kirsty, watching, saw exactly what Dally disliked – the bossiness, the whip held at the ready, the jump-to-it, I'm-in-charge assertiveness. Was she like that herself, when she rode Leo? And then she thought of Alison's parting remark. She didn't think Alison was seriously threatening to move O'Leary elsewhere, not just because of Dally, but all the same it would be a bad time to lose a long-standing customer, with Jay due home in two days.

Alison rode down towards the schooling field, and Lottie rounded on Kirsty.

"There, you see!"

"What?" Kirsty flared.

"You were right first time, and I was wrong – he is peculiar! What do you see in him?"

"Give it a rest, will you? Did you *have* to side with Miss Bossyboots?"

"But Alison was right!" Lottie protested. "He doesn't know anything about horses and yet he thinks he can order people about!"

"He *does* know about horses! That's the whole point. Not about bits and martingales and dressage." Kirsty floundered for words. "He knows what horses are really like. He knows about the horseness of horses."

"The what?"

"I'm going to look at Dorcas and the foal," Kirsty said, giving up. She still had Petronella to groom before the Nellies arrived.

The mare was standing with head lowered towards the foal, who was lying flat in the straw with all four legs stretched out straight. Kirsty's heart thumped for a moment, thinking he had died; then she saw the rise and fall of his rib cage, and the unperturbed mare standing guard. "Isn't he beautiful?" she whispered to Lottie, who had followed. She marvelled at the size of his knees and hocks and fetlocks compared to the small body and miniature hooves. A few hours old, he would already be able to get up and run with the herd if he were a wild horse.

Lottie refused to be deflected. "The way he was in the house – letting you wait on him hand and foot, and hardly a grunt for Thank you! What is he, a cave man?"

"End of subject, I told you! I wonder if I ought to close

this top door, as there are bound to be people around? They shouldn't have people gawping in at them all day."

"All right then, I'll shut up," Lottie said. "But I'm telling you, if he's here when I come back this evening, I'm going *straight home*."

CHAPTER 13

All day, Kirsty felt bad about Dally. It had been unfortunate timing, Lottie coming in so unexpectedly; not Lottie's fault, but it had upset Dally for some reason, making him moody and silent. He didn't have to be like that. Kirsty was beginning to think of him as a difficult horse, one who must be treated kindly and consistently if he were to show his true, generous spirit. He was kind, even considerate; she knew that, though it would be no use trying to explain to Lottie, who had seen only bad grace and yobbishness.

In mid-afternoon, Lottie rode home on Puzzle to help her father for a couple of hours; her mother would drive her back at half-past six to share a meal with Kirsty. Sheila finally left, having spent several hours doting on the foal, taking spools of photographs and hushing everyone who went near; the Nellies had gone to a show, taking the pony in a hired trailer, and wouldn't be back till late. Kirsty fetched a mattress into her room as a makeshift bed for Lottie, tidied up, then decided to ride Leo over to Ravenswood to bring Prince in and do his stable. She folded Dally's black shirt and put it into her rucksack as an excuse for going to look for him.

Dally, besides turning Prince out as she had asked, had done the stable, put down a fresh, perfectly banked-up bed of straw, and filled the haynet and water-bucket. With another excuse to find and thank him, Kirsty put Leo in the empty stable next door and left the two horses neighing at each other across the yard while she went to see if Dally was working in the garden.

No sign of him; but she saw Mrs Bishop and Mrs Hendy sitting together on chairs on the stone patio that ran along the back of the house, where the emerging wisteria flowers hung in bunches against the wall, like ghostly grapes. There was a wrought-iron table between the two women, and a tray with a teapot. They must have seen her riding down the track on Leo; now Mrs Hendy waved, and Kirsty felt obliged to go over and chat. Damn.

She told them about Jay coming home, and about the new foal, all the time fidgeting inside. Mrs Hendy nodded and smiled and said, "Do bring your brother round for a drink, Kirsty, if he can spare the time. I'd like to see him." In spite of the warmth of the afternoon, she wore thick stockings and a tweedy skirt and waistcoat. She made Kirsty think of some cold-blooded creature that had crept out to warm itself on the stones.

"If you're looking for Dally," Mrs Hendy said, "he'll have gone home. He has a half-day on Saturdays."

"Oh, I –" Kirsty was taken aback; how did Mrs Hendy know it was Dally she wanted? "I was going to give him something, that's all. A book," she improvised. "One of my Dad's. He was interested."

"Leave it with me and I'll give it to him in the morning," Mrs Bishop said, logically enough. For once, Kirsty's lie had instantly caught her out.

"No, thanks, but I'll wait and give it to him myself. It's a special copy, a signed one."

Kirsty saw a smile twitch at the corners of Mrs Hendy's mouth. How odd, she thought, that she could deceive nearly everyone, but not an old lady who hardly knew her. She must be careful to give away nothing else. Clearly, though, the two women knew nothing about Dally's secret occupation of the cottage. It was a nuisance, them sitting here. If Dally wasn't working he might be there now, but she could hardly march straight across the lawn and through the rose garden. Excusing herself, she went back to the stables, brought Prince in and fed him, and mounted Leo from the block; then she rode right out of Ravenswood to the road, past the frontage of the house, and turned right again down the track on the far side of the wall, that led to the gardener's cottage. If anyone did happen to see her there, she could say she was looking for a way through to the bridle path that ran alongside the river.

Leo's hooves trod softly on the grassy track. Kirsty caught her breath at the sight of the bluebells, now coming into flower – swathes of them, a wash of mauvy blue that made the whole wood seem to float in haze. The beeches and silver birches had come more fully into leaf since her last visit, casting dappled shade over the pools of blue. The air was full of cool blue scent. People would come to see, if they knew; but the wood was secret and enclosed, with no right of way from the road. It was Dally's private wood. Perhaps, till now, he was the only person who had seen.

The cottage came into view, tucked under the high canopy of leaves. Kirsty looked to see if door or window were open; then her attention was distracted by a leaping cat that flew across the track in a blur of grey and white, and a commotion of birds in the walled garden to her right. She brought Leo to a halt by the wrought-iron gate.

Inside, on the strip of lawn that separated the borders, a fledgling blackbird sat squawking defiance at the cat, which squatted a mere half-metre away, ready to pounce. Two parent birds, helpless, shrieked their alarm calls from the top of the brick wall. Quickly Kirsty dismounted, tied Leo's reins to the paling fence of the cottage and pushed the gate open.

The cat looked round, green eyes darting resentment. The fledgling squawked again and the cat swished its tail, treading with its hind feet for a firm purchase on the ground. Then it sprang. The bird tried to flutter away on wings too short and feeble to do more than carry it a few metres; the cat was upon it, taking it in its mouth. Kirsty saw the yellow gape of the fledgling's beak as it screeched its terror. The parent birds flapped and shrilled in agitation. Shouting, Kirsty ran for the cat, clapping her hands to startle it into dropping the baby bird. For a second the bird fluttered free, but the cat was quicker than Kirsty and seized it again. It turned to face her, growling, with the fledgling clamped in its jaws; then it ran into the border where the rose-bushes were thick and dense. Kirsty went as close as she could, peering through the thorny stems, in the hope of rescuing the bird even now; but it was hopeless. She heard growling, a flutter of feathers, then nothing.

The parent birds were still calling in futile agitation from the wall. She felt a tug of pity for their grief. No, that was silly, sentimental; yet for the moment, grief was all she could see. She had been close enough to see the fledgling's bright eye, the buttercup-yellow corners of its mouth, the stumpy tail and wings that lacked the strength to carry it to safety. Little less than a miracle, it seemed: molecules forming and assembling themselves inside an egg, hatching into a help-less blind creature, then developing into feathers, wings, strong legs and claws. All to end in a cat's jaws the day it left its nest.

Kirsty walked slowly, sorrowfully, back to the gate, where she stopped in disbelief: Leo wasn't there, where she had tied him. His absence was what she saw where there should have been a large horse.

Then, before panic could take her over, she heard the snapping of twigs and saw Dally leading Leo back through the bluebells. She saw boy and horse together against the woodland backdrop, walking between slender beech trunks:

Leo's coat shining rich conker-colours in the dappled sun-light, his ears pricked; Dally smiling, with one hand resting on the horse's neck.

"Hello," she called to him. "It's my fault! I shouldn't have tied him by the reins. Thank God he didn't get out to the road. . ."

"He's broken them," Dally said, showing her the ends of torn leather. "He must have pulled back till they snapped – I'm surprised the fence didn't snap first. What were you doing?"

Kirsty explained about the cat and the birds, her failed rescue. The adult birds were still calling, swooping down to the grass.

"That's Freda. A real hunting cat." Dally tied the broken reins in a knot.

"Ours catch birds sometimes, specially Moth," Kirsty said. "I love the cats, but I do hate them killing things."

"They're cats," Dally said. "That's what cats do."

"I know, but –"

Dally gazed through the gate towards the parent black-birds. "It looks like they're mourning," he said, "but they'll soon forget. What use is mourning to a blackbird? They have to get on with living. It's instinct, protecting their young. They'll go back to their other chicks. They'll even have another brood later in the year. It's survival of the fittest. If all the chicks survived, the world would be swarming with blackbirds." He looked at her. "What did you come for, anyway?"

"I wanted to see you," Kirsty said. "And I've brought your shirt back." She looked for her rucksack, where she had dropped it when she jumped down from Leo's saddle, and found it in the long grasses by the gate.

"Thanks," Dally said. He took the shirt from her and put it on over his T-shirt. "Do you want to bring Leo round the back?"

"The back?"

"There's a fenced garden. More jungle than garden, but he can stay in there for a minute, then you needn't tie him up again. I was out there when I heard him."

Of course, it was far too beautiful a day for him to be sitting in the empty cottage. Kirsty followed him. There was a side gate, just wide enough to lead Leo through. The back garden had a flagged stone path between what must have once been well-tended beds, now rampant with nettles and elder and blackberry suckers. There was a patch of lawn, roughly scythed. Dally closed the gate behind Leo, and Kirsty fastened the reins through the throat-latch of the bridle so that he couldn't get his feet tangled in them. There wouldn't be time to take the reins to the saddler's before Jay came home; they were expensive ones, with rubber grips, that Jay used because Leo took such a strong hold when galloping or jumping. She would have to find some old plain ones for now. Leo snorted and stared prick-eared round his new surroundings, then lowered his head to snatch at mouthfuls of grass, still suspicious.

"He'll be OK, now," Kirsty said, when he had settled. She looked round at Dally, who was carrying something inside. Against the ivy-covered cottage wall she saw a collection of clay models; horses, a human figure, each one about thirty centimetres high, arranged on a dirty crumpled sheet. "What are—"

Whatever they were, Dally didn't want her to see them. He tried to pick up two more, but they were awkward to hold; he put one down and lifted the other, a female figure, with both hands.

"Oh, let me see!" Kirsty crouched to look. "Did you make them? Is this what you do?"

"Yeah. They need firing, only I can't do that, so I thought the sun might bake them a bit." Dally put the clay figure back in its place with the others; then, in a gesture of surrender, he moved away and sat on the doorstep of the open back door. Most of the models were of horses – some lifelike, the work of close observation, others heavily stylized. One was a goose, at a rudimentary stage; the clay was wet with fingermarks.

"Oh, but this is beautiful!" Kirsty stretched out a hand to touch the shoulder of the clay girl. She was slender, crouched, extending one leg as if dipping it in water, trailing the fingers of one hand to test the temperature. Long hair flowed over her shoulders and the clay was modelled to suggest a soft, clinging dress. "She's Ophelia! Is she?"

"If you like." Dally was picking at his fingernails.

"Dally! This is lovely, really lovely! Is this what you do? Are you an art student or something?" Kirsty remembered what Lottie had suggested about Dally taking a year off.

"No!" Dally gave her one of his fierce looks. "You don't have to go to art college. You don't have to have a label on you saying *art student* before you're allowed to start. You can do things on your own! You just do it, and that's how you find out."

"Find out what?"

"Whether you can do it, or not," Dally said, as if it were a stupid question.

"Well, you can! What are you going to do with them? Sell them, get them exhibited somewhere?"

"No! They just are! Why would I want to make money from them? They're not for other people. They're for me."

Kirsty turned to face him. "Why are you so angry?"

"I'm not," he said. Now, he just sounded surly.

"Where d'you get the clay from?" Kirsty tried.

"Art shop in town," Dally answered, more mildly. "I tried digging some up from the ground – the soil's so clayey here – but it wouldn't hold together well enough."

"This girl – is she someone you know?" Kirsty wondered why she was bothering to ask. Dally would never tell her, and it was so easy to offend him.

He picked savagely at a piece of broken nail. "Yes. Knew."

"Who is she? Please tell me!"

Abruptly, Dally stood up and walked over to Leo, who

had long stems of grass tangled round his bit. Dally pulled them out, slobber and all, and wiped his hands on his jeans. When he turned back to Kirsty his face wore a tight, shut-off expression, his mouth in a hard bitter line – almost, she thought in alarm, as if he might cry. She wondered what to do if he did.

"Dally, I'm sorry!" She touched his arm. "I didn't mean—"

"Doesn't matter." But he turned and shrugged her hand off his arm, like a horse twitching away a bothersome fly.

She crouched by the clay models again, looking at the horses. Dally started pulling handfuls of goose-grass from the overgrown bed, taking no notice of her. She didn't know what to say to put things right. Why do I *bother*, she thought? – but then she looked more closely at the clay horses and knew that Dally's difficult nature was what made him fascinating to her, more so every time she met him. From the heavy clay his fingers had shaped beauty and grace, the sweep of a horse's spine, the curve of its neck as it bent to nuzzle a raised hind foot; he had seen those things, and recreated them. He was full of contradictions: churlish yet artistic, aggressive yet tender, devious yet blunt; he was cynical, but with a kind of simple directness that cut through her confusions.

She looked at her watch. "I'll have to go," she said. "Lottie's coming round soon, and I've still got things to do in the yard."

"Don't worry," Dally said, still curt. "I won't turn up and get in the way."

"You wouldn't –" she began, but then thought how awkward it had been this morning in the kitchen, with Lottie turning prim and Dally downright truculent. "Thanks again, anyway, for coming last night. It was really kind of you."

Dally picked up her rucksack and helped her on with it; then he fetched Leo and led him out to the track, adjusted the bridle and tightened the girth and pulled down the stirrups, as if he were her paid groom. Then he gave her a leg-up, throwing her lightly and easily, as before. He knows how to do that, she thought. He can put a lot of things down to common-sense, but he's definitely done that before. People who didn't know how got the timing wrong, or else pitched you too hard, so that you risked sailing right over the horse and down the other side.

"Bye, then," she said. "I'll see you tomorrow. And thanks for letting me see the models. They're great."

He stood looking up at her, squinting into the sun. "Kirsty –"

It was so unusual for him to call her by her name that she noticed it at once.

"I *will* tell you, OK? About the sculptures. Only not now. Some other time." He stroked Leo's shoulder and leaned his face against the horse's neck; then he stepped back. "See you tomorrow."

Kirsty rode away along the track, beside the drifts of bluebells. When she reached the slight curve that hid the cottage from the road, she turned and looked back. Dally was still standing there.

Lottie wanted to watch a TV film that evening, but was also keen to discuss Puzzle's chances in the Welsh Cob class at the county show. "I mean, I know that judge last year hardly looked at us, but he's going so much *better* than last year, don't you think?"

"Yes," said Kirsty, thinking about Dally and the Ophelia girl. She hadn't told Lottie where she had been this afternoon, but she could imagine Lottie's reaction if she did. Lottie would never believe that Dally had never so much as touched her. Apart from giving her the leg-up, and that didn't count; anyone might do that. He was such a touchy person – in more ways than one, she thought, smiling –

"What's funny?" Lottie demanded. "I mean, *you* said how much more supple he was, when you rode him. He ought to be, after all the schooling I've done."

"I know," Kirsty said.

– a touchy person, always touching and stroking horses and cats, yet shying away when she put an apologetic hand on his arm. It must be because of that other girl –

"And there's the in-hand class as well," Lottie said, leafing through the entry booklet. "He might do better in that. You'll come and be groom for me, won't you?"

"Yes," said Kirsty.

– that Ophelia girl. *Knew*, Dally said, not *know*. How odd

155

that she had never thought about Dally and girls at all before, but clearly there was something. The girl had dumped him? Could that be why he was living like a hermit? *Would* he react in such an extreme way to what, after all, happened to most people at some time or other? You couldn't tell, with someone as intense as Dally –

"It's an awful lot in entry money," Lottie said, "but then if I got even third prize. . . And we can have a nice day out. Hey! Why don't you take Leo?"

– but he would tell her about it. At least, tell her about the sculptures, he had said. But that one in particular, the graceful girl. . .

"Well, what about it?" Lottie pursued. "Ridden hunter, working hunter, riding horse – three classes, you could enter him for." She giggled. "Hey, and side-saddle."

"Oh, sure," Kirsty said, paying attention at last. "Me and Leo, at the county show? He'd bolt with me in the ring, or I'll fall off and make an idiot of myself. Anyway, he's Jay's horse, not mine."

"Yes, but if Jay's not here to ride him –"

The phone rang. Kirsty uncurled herself from the sofa to answer it, and muted the TV.

"That's Kirsty, isn't it? Sorry to bother you in the evening." It was Mrs Hendy's voice. "I've just decided that as the weather's so mild now, Prince can be turned out with the cows. Of course that means there'll be no need for you to come any more – I'm sure it's been difficult for you to fit it in, and I've been most grateful. I'll ask Dally to take him down there in the morning, so if you'd like to call in some time, I'll settle up with you? Perhaps with your brother, when he's home?"

"Oh. OK." Kirsty heard her voice hollow with disappointment. She rang off.

"What's the problem?" Lottie said.

"Mrs Hendy doesn't need me round at Ravenswood any more." Kirsty was unable to keep the flatness from her voice.

"Well, what's so bad about that? I'd have thought you'd be *pleased* –" Then Lottie's expression changed to one of tight disapproval. "Oh. Oh, I see."

It rained heavily that night. Kirsty, awake, listened to the distant rumblings of thunder, the hiss of rain; it sounded like a real summer storm, the sort that usually came after days of unbroken hot weather. She watched for lightning, saw sheets of it flash at her window, with a sudden strobe effect; the thunder crackled nearer.

Lottie was sleeping through it, breathing deeply. Kirsty thought of Dally. She knew that he was awake too, watching the storm with his cottage door open: feeling the crackle of air, smelling the wet grass.

CHAPTER 14

Lottie went home for Sunday lunch, which was always a family occasion at the Holcrofts', with a traditional roast. Kirsty was invited, but was too busy getting everything ready for Jay's arrival next day – that was the excuse she gave. After making herself a cheese sandwich and eating it between kitchen and stableyard, she cycled round to Ravenswood. If Mrs Hendy saw her, she could say she had come for her money. In any case, Prince's stable would need to be thoroughly cleaned out.

The weather was cool today, the air moist after the night's rain. The house looked deserted – no one sitting on the patio, no one in the garden. It was lunchtime, and presumably Mrs Hendy would be eating her meal in the lonely splendour of her dining-room. Kirsty went to the stables first, and found the stable already bare, smelling of disinfectant, with the water-bucket and manger scrubbed out. Dally must have done it.

She cycled back past the house, past Mrs Hendy's sitting-room window, and was alerted by the old lady tapping on the glass, beckoning her round to the front door. Reluctantly, Kirsty went.

"I thought I saw you just now. You needn't have worried, I asked Dally to see to everything down there. But as you're here, I'll pay you up to date." Mrs Hendy gave Kirsty a folded note from the saucer by the Chinese vase. The tiled hallway struck cold after the warmth of the sunshine outdoors; Kirsty wondered why she didn't spend more time outside. Then the old lady said, "I must go down and see my bluebells. They'll be coming out now. Have you seen them, in the wood?"

"No!" Kirsty said, too quickly.

"Do go and have a look, if you've got time. They're a wonderful sight. Go through the rose garden and out of the far gate. I think I'll go this afternoon if it stays dry."

"It'll be a bit muddy," Kirsty said, "after all the rain in the night. Didn't you hear it?"

"Yes. I've got wellingtons, though."

Did she know? Was there a knowing glint in the hooded dark eyes? Kirsty put her money in her pocket and said, "I'll see you next week, with Jay."

"Thank you, Kirsty. You've been very reliable. I hope I can call on you again in the autumn?"

Kirsty couldn't think as far ahead as autumn. She said yes and goodbye, and went back to her bicycle, her head full of the urgency of telling Dally that Mrs Hendy might come walking in the woods this afternoon. She bumped her bike down the muddy track to the cottage, breathing the cool bluebell-scented air.

It was all shut up; the front door locked, no window open. She went round to the back. Unless Mrs Hendy came round here and wondered about the scythed grass and the hoof-prints, there was nothing to notice. Suddenly afraid that Dally had packed up and gone, Kirsty peered through the rain-streaked window. Inside, she could see his sleeping-bag, his things laid out, his clay sculptures by the far wall. Mrs Hendy would see them too, if she looked in.

But probably she wouldn't. Not if she were coming to gaze at bluebells. She looked too frail to walk far; she was unlikely to get sidetracked.

Where was he? Where did he go? Kirsty walked across the wet grass of the rose garden, and looked out towards the lake. Freda, the grey-and-white cat, sat by the base of the topiary peacock, washing her paws.

"Nasty thing," Kirsty said, seeing not the demure paw-washer but the growling savage with a bird in its jaws.

She thought about leaving Dally a note, pushing it under the door: *I came to see you.* In her pocket she had an old shopping list. Nothing to write with, though; she would have to come back later.

In frustration she cycled home, and found the yard entrance blocked by a police car.

Her thoughts raced. Leo, Dorcas, the fillies, she thought wildly, imagining a gaping wound, a shattered bone, a horse bleeding to death alone in a field. There were two officers, one sitting in the car, the other, in shirtsleeves, talking to

Alison, who was holding O'Leary. Then she saw that Alison was smiling, and the officer in the car absently drumming his fingers on the steering wheel.

"Here's Kirsty," Alison said, as Kirsty pulled level with the car.

"What's happened?"

"Kirsty Millen?" the officer said. He was youngish and handsome, with bright blue eyes beneath his peaked cap. "Are your parents at home?"

"No. My mother doesn't live here. My dad'll be home later. What's happened?"

"There's been another attempted attack on horses, locally," the officer said. "But this time we've got a description. The owner managed to see the two boys and chase them off. Stud farm over near Lower Fyfield, it was."

"Two boys?"

"Yes, not much to go on – two lads of around sixteen, he says. They were out in his field early this morning, trying to corner a mare and foal they'd separated from the rest. He didn't actually see a weapon but he was certain they were up to no good. You haven't seen any strange boys around here?"

"No. No one," Kirsty said. Alison caught her eye, and looked away.

"We're advising all horse owners to keep a careful eye out," said the policeman. "Is this your own horse, Miss Wilcox?" he added to Alison.

"Alison. Yes, that's right," Alison said, with a bright sociable smile. "His name's O'Leary. And no one had better try to hurt him."

"Oirish, is he?" The policeman ventured forward and gingerly patted O'Leary's nose. "A fine-looking animal." He flicked his eyes up and down Alison as if including her in the compliment.

"Thank you!" Alison said, almost simpering. Kirsty could see that she was rather taken with the officer's blue eyes and handsome face. If they were going to stand here *flirting* with each other, she had better things to do. She went to park her bike.

"Just a moment, Miss Millen."

She stopped.

"Ask your dad to give me a call when he gets home, could you? I'd like to have a word with him, just in case."

"He won't know anything," Kirsty said. "I run the yard, not him. He doesn't have anything to do with it."

The officer looked taken aback. "You're very young to be running a place like this." He obviously thought she was about fourteen. "All the same, I'd like to speak to your father."

"OK, I'll tell him," Kirsty said.

"And do ring me at the police station if you see anything suspicious. Anything at all. Ask for Keith Schofield, DC Keith Schofield. Thanks for your help. Bye." He nodded at Kirsty, smiled at Alison, and got into the passenger seat.

Kirsty heard the whine of voices on the radio as he opened the door; he waved as the other man reversed the car and pulled out of the yard. Alison led O'Leary into his stable and closed the door. She still hadn't forgiven Kirsty for yesterday morning.

Two boys, Kirsty was thinking. Lads, the officer had called them. That made it sound almost acceptable – lads having fun, getting up to mischief. But this wasn't laddishness. This was deliberate cruelty, hurting animals for kicks, choosing horses as victims because they were vulnerable. Because they were highly sensitive, because they could feel pain and terror. Kirsty shivered.

She intended to bike back to find Dally at some stage of the evening, but instead found herself waiting for the vet. When she took Dorcas her feed, she found the foal lying down, dull and listless. She fetched the thermometer and found that his temperature was considerably higher than normal. Examining him, she saw that he had severe diarrhoea; his slim buttocks and the underside of his tail were coated with strong-smelling, semi-liquid faeces. She phoned the vet, then Sheila, who drove over straight away, and they spent an anxious few hours.

Her father arrived home, relaxed and congenial from his course. It had gone well, he said, and he'd been invited to a Literature Festival in Wales later in the summer. He came down to see the foal, made vague sympathetic noises and went back indoors to check his e-mail. It was nearly nine before the vet arrived, apologizing for being late. The foal's problem, she said after a quick examination, was a common one, not really much to worry about, though they'd need to keep an eye on him.

"It's a reaction to the mare's milk. A lot of foals get it, till their system adjusts. I'm giving him something to settle his stomach, and you'll need to wash his bottom and tail a few times every day, and put Vaseline on to stop the soreness. Ring me if it doesn't clear up in a day or two."

Kirsty, very tired, went indoors to tell her father, and found him watching a film.

"A pot of coffee would go down well," he said.

"OK." Kirsty made it, brought it in on a tray; they drank it together, and he told her about his course, what the students were like, and about some of the unspeakably dire novels they'd brought with them. He told Kirsty about showing them the beginning of *The Damage Done,* letting them read it in parts, how complimentary they were.

"I'm really beginning to believe in it! I shall finish it now, no trouble, in spite of the break in routine. Well, I'm about to turn in." He got up, yawning, and turned off the TV. "Early start tomorrow. Are you coming to Heathrow with me?"

"I can't," Kirsty said, annoyed that he didn't *know* she couldn't; not with all the horses to do, and now the foal needing extra care. She was grateful for having such an obvious excuse; the thought of plate glass and escalators, signs and announcements and people, made her stomach churn. For the last week, her phobia had begun to slide out of view; no one had expected her to go anywhere, or do anything she didn't want to. But the panicky feelings were still there inside, coiled, dormant, full of vigour. How long, she thought wearily, how long am I going to be like this? Am I stuck with it for life?

She cleared up the coffee things and washed the cat dishes. She thought of Dally sitting at the table, saying, *I think he's a shit, your father.* She hadn't wanted to agree with him then, and she didn't want to now. But she knew. She had known for certain since May last year, and now . . . Graham had talked about his own weekend, his success; he had shown mild interest in the foal. But he hadn't asked about Lottie staying, or how the foaling had gone, or whether there was any more news of the horse attacker – he hadn't asked about anything. Kirsty, expecting to have to conceal the fact that Dally had stayed overnight, had no need to conceal anything. Her father wasn't interested enough to bother asking.

She thought about going upstairs to confront him, but decided that she was too tired, and didn't want a row the night before Jay came home.

Tomorrow. Just a few hours away.

Jay came straight down to the yard to find her, crushing her in a bear hug that left her breathless. "Mouse!" He held her at arm's length to look at her. "How's my favourite sister? You look great!"

She laughed, reinflating her lungs, looking at him. He was tanned and fit, his thick hair cut shorter than when he had left; he was physically like their father, but slimmer and more animated.

"Come and see! Let me show you everything!"

"Lead on, MacMouse."

She took him on a tour of the yard, showing him the mare and foal, the clean, orderly stables, and lastly Leo. She had been up early, giving Leo a special grooming; now he looked wonderful, a real class horse, his summer coat shining with health, his hooves oiled, mane and tail trimmed. Jay went in and slapped the horse's neck.

"How are you, old man? Missed me? We'll ride out, later," he said to Kirsty, bending to run his fingers down the suspect tendon. "The jet lag can wait – I've been looking forward to this. This looks fine! No puffiness at all. Is there something for you to ride? O'Leary?"

"It'll have to be Patches," Kirsty said. Alison's coolness made it impossible to ask to borrow O'Leary.

They walked back to the house for breakfast. "You're doing a fantastic job!" Jay said, his arm across Kirsty's shoulders. "I knew there was no need to worry about anything, with you in charge. You're enjoying it, aren't you?"

"Yes, I am. It's just that –"

"What?"

No. It wasn't the time. "It'll be even better when you're back for good," she said.

Jay laughed, crouching to stroke Moth by the back door. Kirsty cooked breakfast – the whole lot, bacon, eggs, sausages and tomatoes, to welcome Jay home. Graham came down, and the three of them sat round the table talking. Mostly, Jay talked about the Connecticut ranch, the Berkshire mountains and the waterfalls, his trip to New York, and Matt McPherson's Olympic hope, a horse called Omaha Dream.

"And Emma?" Kirsty prompted. "What about Emma?"

"Oh, she's great," Jay said. "Going into real estate with her father." Emma had recently graduated from an Ivy League university.

"Smart girl." Graham poured more coffee. "That's where the money is."

"But – you and Emma – you're OK, aren't you?" Kirsty said.

Jay looked at her. "Sure. Why not?"

He's starting to sound American, Kirsty thought. "You haven't said much about her, that's all."

"Give me time, Mousie! I've only just got here and I've been talking non-stop! There's so much to tell you. Emma's fine, just a bit disappointed she couldn't come this time, that's all."

"This time?"

"Well, she loved it so much last summer. Seeing the sights

of London – she couldn't get enough." Jay laughed. "I've still got the blisters from traipsing round Westminster, the Tower, St. Paul's, every single museum – you name it, we did it. Hey, Mouse, d'you fancy a day in London? I won't dare go back till I've bought something special for Em. Something really *British*. We could go and see Mum, as well. I said I would."

Stalling, Kirsty considered Emma's present. "An Arran sweater? Americans like those, don't they? You could get one by mail order, next-day delivery."

"You don't fancy a day out?"

"I can't! How can I leave the yard? Especially with the foal not well. . ."

"Oh, someone else can keep any eye on him! What about Sheila? It's her foal, after all. What's she going to call him?"

"She hasn't made her mind up. Herbert, she calls him at the moment. He'll be Herbert for life if she doesn't give him a proper name soon."

The house felt so different with Jay at home. He filled it with energy and enthusiasm, going upstairs two at a time, noticing every small change, putting on an American accent, telling Kirsty about the people and horses on the ranch. He had brought her a souvenir from the Empire State Building – a plastic model, with King Kong waving from the top. "Totally naff, but I couldn't resist! Keep it till you come and see for yourself."

Later, he and Kirsty rode out together. Jay, from Leo's saddle, laughed at Kirsty as she led out the fat piebald, Patches.

"Bit of a comedown for you. Good old Patches. He looks as if he should be pulling a milk float."

Kirsty mounted, adjusted her stirrups. "Don't say things like that in front of him! He's a dear old boy. And I'd have never learned to ride without him."

But, after Leo's height and scope, riding Patches felt like sitting astride a barrel. Instead of the expanse of shoulder and neck in front of the saddle, the pony's short curved ears – one white, one black – bobbed close to Kirsty's face. When Jay pushed into a trot towards the village, she tried to adapt to Patches' stumpy stride as he clopped after the bigger horse.

"I feel like a little kid!" she called to Jay. "And you look so high up –"

"Leo's great, though. It's good to be back. I thought of going through Brackett's Wood, if it's not too muddy up there?"

"Yes, fine." It was months since Kirsty had been on such a long ride. She watched Jay with pleasure, admiring the way he rode: sitting easily, deeply in the saddle, the reins in one hand. When he came back they could do this every day. It would be nice to have a horse for herself, the only problem being that there was no money to buy one. Maybe she could find a horse to loan, or one that needed schooling. With Jay sharing the work, she would have more time for a project of her own.

A muddy, rutted track led into the Forestry Commission wood. The edges were planted with young deciduous trees in long grass; farther in, the forest closed on the track, dense-packed spruces and pines whose interlaced branches held coolness. Kirsty smelled the sharp tang of resin, and Jay said, "This smell, it's just like the Berkshires. Takes me straight back there. Come on, let's go – I need to shake off that jet lag."

Without waiting for an answer, he spurred Leo into a canter. The horse needed no encouragement. Patches, taking a surprisingly strong hold, set off in keen pursuit. When the track opened out and became grassy, with a slight uphill incline, Jay let Leo lengthen his stride, moving up a gear. Kirsty thought of Leo's strained tendon – she had been taking it so easily up to now, all walking exercise with a little slow trotting. "Jay –" she shouted, but the big horse was already well ahead, and Patches, with his much shorter stride, straining to catch up. The speed, even on gallumph-ing Patches, was exhilarating, the trees a passing blur, the pony's breath coming in excited snorts, his hooves pound-ing. Leo was quite out of sight around a bend in the track; Kirsty saw the skidding hoofprints, and smelled the churned earth.

Jay had come to a halt where the track narrowed and became stony. Leo, his neck dark with sweat, curvetted and pranced as the pony slithered to a halt. Jay sat easily, smiling, his feet dangling out of the stirrups. "That shook the cobwebs away! He went like the clappers when I put my foot on the throttle."

"I hope he's OK," Kirsty said anxiously, looking at the suspect foreleg. "I should have told you, I've only been riding him quietly till now –"

"He's fine," Jay said. "I had a good look at it before we came out. Don't *worry* about everything!"

But I do worry, Kirsty thought as they rode more quietly along the leaf-fringed track at the edge of the wood. Worrying's what I do. How can you not, when you're looking after animals with injuries and diarrhoea, animals that can get themselves caught in fences, or hurt themselves on nails, or get colic and die from twisted guts? To say nothing of *people*, and what they might do. Not worrying was what Dad was good at – perhaps Jay took after him. If you behaved as if problems didn't exist, then maybe they didn't.

They rode back through the village, the two sets of hooves clattering in the quiet street. As they passed the shop, the door opened suddenly with its jingle of bells. Leo shied, skittering across the road; Jay calmed him and rode on. Kirsty, behind, found herself face to face with Dally, who was standing in the shop doorway with a carrier-bag. She brought Patches to a halt. The pony resisted, wanting to follow Leo.

Kirsty felt herself tingling with nervousness. "Oh . . . I looked for you yesterday!" she told Dally. "At the –" she lowered her voice – "cottage, but you weren't there. And then I had to wait for the vet. Otherwise I would've. . ."

Dally said nothing, looking at the pony, then down the street at Jay, who had turned Leo and was riding back towards them.

"When shall I see you?" Kirsty said quickly. "Tomorrow, if I can? Jay's staying, he only got home today. . ."

He nodded; then Jay brought Leo back to stand next to Patches. Kirsty saw the strength and beauty of Leo's muscular, arched neck, the lift and fall of his mane, and then she saw what Dally saw; Jay's spurs, the way he had Leo collected and fired up, making the horse flex his jaw and accept the bit. Leo was unsettled after his gallop, wanting to fidget, sweat creaming on his neck. When Kirsty rode him, he walked quietly home on a long rein.

"This is Jay, my brother," Kirsty explained. "Jay, this is Dally, who works for Mrs Hendy."

"Hi!" Jay said. "Pleased to meet you."

Dally lifted his chin, unsmiling.

"Dally looks after the gardens." Kirsty felt the need to fill the silence.

"Full-time job, I should imagine," Jay said pleasantly; and then, when Dally still said nothing, "Let's get these horses home then, Mouse."

Kirsty tried to catch Dally's eye, but he was watching Jay as the two horses moved off. "Bye," she called, and Dally turned away in the direction of Ravenswood.

"Man of few words," Jay remarked. He checked Leo, brought him to a half-halt, then relaxed his hands to allow him to walk on again. Leo stretched his neck and walked with a long stride, feeling for the bit, settling. Dally didn't understand about riding, Kirsty thought; Leo, properly ridden, looked like a horse fit for Badminton or Aintree. When she rode him, she let him slop along anyhow.

"You can ride him tomorrow, in the schooling field," Jay said, glancing at her. "I'd like to see how he goes for you."

"But I've never schooled him before," Kirsty objected.

"There's a first time for everything. You can have the sole benefit of my expert tuition, fresh from Matt McPherson himself."

"Oh, I forgot! Mrs Hendy wants you to go round for sherry. She's mentioned it about six times. I think you're her blue-eyed boy."

Jay pulled a face. "God, do I have to? Can't you tell her I've got too much on, like tidying my sock drawer?"

CHAPTER 15

Three-fifteen in the morning, and Kirsty was lying in bed, wide awake.

She had been jolted into consciousness by one of those heart-stopping moments, flung violently back into her own body. Her mind was filled with a blackness that was already unidentifiable, slipping from her grasp.

Now that she was awake, the thought of Jay in the next room calmed her. She was fully alert, and sleep was impossible. She lay for a while listening to the house's creaking and gurgling noises, wondering why they didn't seem in the least threatening when she knew she wasn't alone; then she became aware of sounds from downstairs.

Jay. The TV. His body clock was all wrong; for him it was only ten o'clock in the evening. Kirsty put on her dressing-gown and socks, and went downstairs.

"Hi!" Jay was sprawled across the sofa, feet over the armrest, watching a video. "It's no good. I thought if I didn't let myself sleep during the day it'd get me back to normal, but it's not working so far."

Kirsty sat in the big armchair, curling her legs up inside her dressing-gown for warmth.

"Didn't wake you up, did I?" He flipped back the ring-pull on a can of lager.

"No. I often wake up and then can't sleep again."

"Yeah?" He took a swig. "Why's that?"

Kirsty hesitated. It was the cue for the conversation she had often imagined having with Jay: I get frightened. Frightened of being frightened. Of what my brain might do to scare me, in the middle of the night. She leaned her head against the chair back, formulating her opening sentence, anticipating the relief of sharing her fears with someone sympathetic. Then it occurred to her that she couldn't tell Jay, not now, when he was about to go back to the States and leave her in charge of the yard for another four months. He thought she was coping; he needed to believe it.

"It's nothing, it doesn't matter," she said.

"Mm?" Jay glanced back from the TV, and she saw that he had given up waiting for an answer. The screen was filled with fast action shots of a car chase. Close-ups of narrowed eyes and hands gripping steering wheels alternated with giddy panning shots, all to the background of squealing tyres and tense music. She closed her eyes, letting the sounds fuzz in her brain.

She woke to dawn light through the curtains and the sound of Jay's breathing. He was deeply asleep on the sofa, lying flat on his back with an arm over his face; one hand trailed to the floor, with the remote control still in it. The TV was on, a programme about Russian literature. Kirsty stretched out her cramped legs, turned off the television and gently placed the remote control on the coffee table. Then she went upstairs to get dressed.

Late in the afternoon, Tatjana phoned, back from Berlin.

"How was it?" Kirsty asked.

"Great! I'm completely knackered, but we had a fantastic time. Tell you all about it tonight, if you like! How about coming to the pub? Ross and Ollie are coming, and Ella, and a couple of others"

"Oh sorry, I can't!" Kirsty had the security of a genuine excuse this time. "Jay's here, he only came back yesterday, and Dad's making us a special dinner tonight. Why don't you come round tomorrow?"

Tatjana agreed, and Kirsty rang off. Her father was slicing lemons and the kitchen was full of intoxicating smells – he was making his special spiced chicken. When he cooked Indian-style, he liked to make a big performance of it, spending most of the day in the kitchen, grinding cumin seeds, blending spices, stirring and tasting and making dozens of relishes and sambals; Kirsty was used to eating leftovers for the next week. Jay, giving in to his body's skewed sense of time, had gone upstairs to sleep, but when he came down Kirsty was going to ride Leo in the schooling field.

"You could have invited Tatjana round for the meal," Graham said. "Phone her back, if you want."

"Could I?"

Kirsty reached for the handset, then paused, thinking of the four of them sitting round the table. Tat would have interesting, clever things to say, she would charm Jay just as she charmed Graham; it would be Tatjana's evening. No. Kirsty wanted the evening to herself, just the three of them, family.

Sometimes she disliked what she found in herself.

"I forgot," she told her father. "Tat's going out."

It was nearly seven by the time Jay came downstairs, rumpled and yawning. "God, sorry, Mouse," he said, rubbing his eyes. "I just crashed out. Have you got Leo ready?"

"Do you still want to bother?"

"Sure! He ought to have some exercise – he's been standing in his stable all day. Go and get your things. I'm going to take a quick shower to wake myself up."

Half an hour later, Kirsty was riding the big horse in front of Jay's critical gaze: settling him into a collected trot, circling, changing the rein across the diagonal of the school, extending. Jay, like an instructor, called out commands to her. "Now bring him back, but with impulsion, get his back legs under him – that's better. A circle at the far end, then into a canter at C."

Kirsty, who had never ridden Leo like this before, felt him supple and obedient underneath her, dropping his nose to her feel on the reins, lengthening his stride in answer to slight pressure from her legs. He made her feel she was riding well. It was Jay's training that made him go so well, she knew; nothing to do with her limited ability as a rider. But she saw Jay looking pleased, and after a while he told her to walk on a long rein. He started to pull out poles from under the fence at the side. "OK, we'll see what you make of a little jump."

A *little jump* wasn't quite how Kirsty would have described it; Jay made a spread fence, from barrels and poles, that would have looked formidable from the back of a smaller horse. He stood back, and Kirsty circled at a canter a few times before putting Leo at the jump. With ears pricked, he lengthened his stride and sailed over in a smooth bound; Kirsty patted him, relieved that it had been so easy.

"Fine, but I'd like to see you having a bit more to do with it," Jay said. "Shorten your reins next time, see your stride, don't just sit there. Be a bit more assertive."

He made her jump the fence six more times before he was satisfied. Then he took a packet of Polo mints from his jeans pocket and gave one to Leo, holding it flat on his palm. Leo waffled it up eagerly, and Jay slapped his neck.

"Great! You look good on him. We'll do that again."

Kirsty dismounted, ran the stirrups up the leathers and loosened the girth. She felt a swell of pride at having done better than she expected, at having ridden well enough to please Jay. She stroked Leo's nose. She heard his back teeth crunching the Polo mints, smelled his minty breath.

"You want me to ride him like this regularly now? So that he's really fit for when you come back?" Kirsty asked.

There was a pause. Then Jay said, "Not exactly." He took the reins over the horse's head, and presented them to Kirsty. "I want to give him to you."

She took them, not understanding. "Give him to me? Why? He's your horse, you've done all the work – you've got plans for him, for competing, eventing –"

"Mouse." Jay put his arm round her shoulders. "The point is – well, I don't know how to say this, so I'll just say it – I won't be coming back."

"You're not –"

"I've decided to stay on in the States," Jay said gently. "Matt's offered me a job when this year's up, and Em and I are going to get married. There's a staff house goes with the job."

Kirsty pulled free, facing him. "You can't! You've got a job here! A place of our own, a yard – it's what you've always wanted!"

Jay looked down and scraped the toe of his boot on the dried mud. "I know. It *was* what I wanted. But now there's Emma, and – well, things are different. We've got to be together, and she won't come and live in England – there's all her family in Connecticut—"

"Oh, so you can leave *your* family! No problem for you!"

Jay unfastened the buckle of Leo's drop noseband, not meeting Kirsty's eye. "Come on, Kirsty. Don't make this hard for me."

"Have you told Dad yet?" she demanded.

"Yes, I have. We talked about it at lunchtime, after you'd gone out."

"And what did he say?"

"Oh, he was a bit disappointed at first, I think, but he could see what a good opportunity I've got out there. He soon came round."

"And now you want me to come round," Kirsty said flatly. "You're giving me Leo as a consolation prize. You think that makes it OK to throw our plans out of the window – *my* plans as well as yours, in case you'd forgotten. Changed them without asking. What about me? What am I supposed to do?"

Jay said, "You're doing so well here. Brilliantly. You're all set up – the yard, owners, now a fabulous horse of your own. What more could you want? You can run the place, you've proved you can. I wouldn't suggest you did it, unless I thought you could cope. You don't need me."

Angrily, Kirsty started to lead Leo back in. "It's not the same! I've worked and worked because I thought we were going to do this together! You're the one with the training, the knowledge –" She fumbled with the latch of the paddock gate. "I can't believe you're just going to walk out like this. I won't believe it. I don't want to do it on my own!"

She thought of mucking out stables, getting up in the cold winter dawn, trying to please the livery owners and balance the books – all on her own, with her father not caring and Jay not there. What was the point? Jay was the one with ambitions, with experience, with expertise. Without him, she was just a drudge.

Jay followed behind. "Mouse, do be reasonable –"

"Reasonable!" she flung at him. "You're telling me to be reasonable! After you've messed me about – cleared off and found something more exciting to do! *Oh, never mind Kirsty, she doesn't matter, she can manage.* Well, I can't! I'm not going to."

She led Leo into his stable, unbuckled his girth and dumped the saddle on the half-door, almost hitting Jay in the face with it. "I hate Emma!" she burst out. "It's her fault, taking you away! She's so selfish – if she really loved you she'd come to live in England. It's not fair!"

"Don't try to blame Emma." Jay lifted the trailing girth and folded it over the seat of the saddle. "It's not only her – it's the job with Matt. I'd be mad to turn it down, just to—" He realized, too late, what he had said. "I mean, to –"

Kirsty glared at him. "Oh, *just*! *Just* to come back here! *Just* to keep your promise! I see what you mean, all right." She turned away from him, dragging her feet in the straw. She took off Leo's bridle; then she leaned against the horse with her face in his mane. Hot tears blurred her eyes. She tried to blink them back.

"Kirsty, come on." Jay entered the stable and put a hand on her shoulder. "Don't take it like this. Come indoors and we'll talk about it. We're not abandoning you, honestly – you can come over and stay, as soon as you like, and we'll come home sometimes –"

We. It was *we* now, Jay and Emma.

"Leave me alone," Kirsty said, through gritted teeth. She shook his hand off, ducking under Leo's neck. "I wouldn't dream of getting in the way of you and wonderful Matt and wonderful perfect Emma. I'm *just* Kirsty, remember? Just your little sister, who can stay at home and do all the work."

"Oh, now you're just being pathetic," Jay said, his voice hardening. "I'm giving you my horse, I've told you I'm getting married, said you can come over and stay – not a word of thanks, or congratulations. I'll talk to you when you're in a better mood."

"Don't count on it!" Kirsty hurled after him as he left the stable.

Her words echoed in the quiet of the stable when Jay had gone. Leo pulled at his haynet, unconcerned by the shouting, his jaws moving roundly on the hay. Kirsty rubbed him down, taking a very long time. With Jay no longer there, she felt more angry than tearful; she didn't know how to go into the kitchen and sit down to appreciate Dad's Indian cookery.

No. Jay would want to discuss his plans, his glittering future. She couldn't sit and eat with them, couldn't listen. For all her skill at pretending, it would be an act quite beyond her.

She put Leo's tack away and went up to the house. In the kitchen her father was stirring rice, in a cloud of fragrant, spicy smells. Jay, sitting at the kitchen table with a can of lager in front of him, smiled at her in a tight, let's-pretend-everything's-normal way. For the first time, Kirsty saw a resemblance to her mother; she had always thought him more like Graham. "Sit down and have a drink!" he said, patting the seat next to him. "Dad's opening a bottle of wine "

"I'm going up for a shower."

"Food ready in fifteen minutes, Kirsty," her father called after her.

She didn't answer. Upstairs, she opened the door to her father's study and sat down in his revolving chair. His computer was turned on, the screen-saver making a swirly coloured pattern, like a kaleidoscope.

I hate them, Kirsty thought. Both of them.

CHAPTER 16

At the time, she had told herself that she would never forgive her father. But she had; because time had passed – nearly a year of it – and, in the end, it became too difficult to stay hostile towards someone she shared a house with. She had simply forgotten, day by day, to be angry with him.

And now she was angry with herself, for forgetting, for allowing herself to mellow and to appear to forgive. They both do exactly as they like, she thought, Dad and Jay. They're both the same. They see a chance and they take it, no matter how it might hurt anyone else.

June, last year. Kirsty, in school uniform, her bag bumping on her back, was cycling along the lane towards Bramblings, between hedgerows starred with dog-roses. Going home in the middle of the day gave her an odd, incongruous holiday feeling, in spite of the science exam she had just done and tomorrow's geography to revise for. The GCSEs had brought study leave and a break from routine.

She parked her bike by the back door, looking down towards the stableyard. Jay wouldn't be here, it was one of the days he spent instructing at the posh equitation centre at

Wolverton, but she thought she might groom Leo for him in case he wanted to ride out later, and bring Patches in for herself. If she spent the afternoon on geography, she could award herself an hour's riding. It was important to relax; her Year Head had said so. Work for an hour or two, doing something specific, then give yourself a reward.

Kirsty went into the house. Through the kitchen, into the main room.

Then she heard voices in the room above. Soft, murmuring voices; a low giggle. A creak of bed springs. In her father's room, in the room that had been her parents'. Kirsty listened.

Mum's come back, she thought, her heart filling; come back to stay. She's had enough of that awful Phil and she's coming back to us.

She was half-shocked and half-amused. In the middle of the day! Couldn't they *wait*? It wasn't the time to go upstairs, not now. She went back to the kitchen and made herself a sandwich. When she heard one of them in the shower overhead, then it would be safe to go up. She poured a glass of milk and sat down to eat her sandwich, flicking through the local paper. Mum's here, Mum's here, she sang inside her head; it meant everything was back to normal.

Footsteps coming down the stairs. Kirsty carried on pretending to read; she would surprise them by pretending to be surprised.

Her father's voice, gruff, awkward: "Oh, Kirsty. What are you doing here?"

And behind him, not Mum, but Suzanne – a livery owner, a girl only a little older than Kirsty, a girl with dark hair and brown eyes and high, firm breasts and, now, a face flushed with embarrassment. Kirsty stared, taking in the two of them freeze-framed in the doorway.

Her father was the first to speak. "We've been up in the study. I've been showing Suzanne how to use the Internet."

Suzanne fastened a button on her shirt and pulled the hem down over her hips. "Yes, isn't it great? I never knew how much you can do. . ."

"And to think I could have walked straight in," Kirsty said. She didn't recognize the voice that was speaking. It was hard-edged, coming from somewhere deep in her chest. "So you're on study leave, like me?" she asked Suzanne.

"Yes," Suzanne said, on a puzzled up-note.

"I wonder what you've been studying," Kirsty said, in that same hard voice that seemed to be someone else's. She looked straight at her father.

"Kirsty—"

"Oh, don't say anything! I don't want to hear it –" Her normal voice had come back now, shaking, out of control. She blundered to her feet and out of the kitchen, and stormed down to the yard looking for Jay. Suzanne's pony, a pretty chestnut Arab called Basil, was looking over his stable door. No Jay, of course not, Kirsty remembered; she would have to go over to Wolverton to find him. She ran back for her bike. Her father, serious-faced, was coming down the path to find her.

"Kirsty, listen –" He tried to take her arm.

She wrenched herself free and turned to face him with hot, angry eyes. "Don't touch me! Don't come anywhere near me!"

She grabbed her bike, glimpsing Suzanne in the kitchen doorway, wide-eyed and shocked. Then she was away and cycling, standing on the pedals, pumping as fast as she could. The dog-roses blurred and swam in her eyes, distant as stars. Her head was full of Suzanne and Dad. Flirty Suzanne who was only sixteen, the same as Kirsty. Suzanne, who had come to ride her pony but found something more exciting to do, upstairs in Dad's bedroom. The horses brought a nice bonus for him, all those girl owners in tight jodhpurs and clingy T-shirts. Suzanne probably thought she had made a conquest – an interesting older man, handsome, a writer who did mysterious things up in his study; Dad had done his ego some good by pulling a sexy sixteen-year-old. He was too fascinated by Suzanne to bother remembering Kirsty's exam timetable – had probably forgotten that she had exams at all. She changed gear for the hill out of the village, pedalling hard. Why do they have to *do* it, she thought: why do they have to have all this sex? Mum and Phil, Jay and Emma, Dad and Clare, now Dad and Suzanne – they're all at it. It gets in the way, it spoils things, it takes them away from me –

Her fury had carried her almost as far as Wolverton, to Jay, when she had a better idea.

Instead of taking the lane towards the riding school, she rode back towards school, turning into the housing estate where Ross lived. She had been there before, often, after school, at weekends: at first with a group of friends; recently, since she had been going out with Ross, on her own. Ross opened the door, wearing jeans and his school shirt hanging loose; his feet were bare.

He looked at Kirsty with his easy smile. "Hi! Didn't know you were coming round."

"I thought we might do some revision together," Kirsty said.

He was alone in the house; music thumped from upstairs, from his room. Kirsty followed him up. *They all do it, and so can I,* she thought; here was Ross, here was his bed, here was an opportunity.

There was nothing to it. All she had to do was sprawl on the bed and pull Ross down beside her, kiss him with an eagerness that surprised him, unbutton his shirt and slide it off his shoulders. He responded willingly, helping her off with her clothes, fumbling with buttons and her bra-clip, then lying on top of her and parting her legs with his knee. He was so easily led, so gullible; he thought it was for him.

It hurt more than she expected. Ross, thrusting, gasped against her shoulder, not noticing. Kirsty, expecting the climactic, blissful communion she had seen a hundred times in films, was disappointed; he was remote from her, engrossed in his own sensation. The room smelled of sex and sweat. He rolled his weight off her and lay gazing at the ceiling while his breathing slowed; then he turned to her in concern and said, "God, I never – you know – used a rubber. What if you're pregnant?"

"You didn't think of that five minutes ago," Kirsty said. Now that it was over, she was trembling; shocked, as if she was an accident victim. She could hear it in her voice. Ross, now that the brief moment of passion was over, looked like a kid whose silly behaviour had gone too far and was now called to account for himself at the headteacher's office. Kirsty could have laughed at him.

"No, but seriously!"

"We'll have to get married," Kirsty said flippantly. "Actually, I'd quite like a baby. Wouldn't you?"

Ross looked at her appalled. "Kirsty! Are you off your trolley?"

"Probably. I'm going home now." Shivering, she reached for her clothes. Five minutes later she was on her bike and cycling home, thinking that she ought to feel transformed, initiated into the mysteries of adulthood; instead she only felt sore.

I hope I am pregnant. Serve them all right.

She never did tell Jay about finding their father with Suzanne. Her own shameful secret became inseparable from his.

Resentment was a coiled snake inside her, a snake that stirred and stretched at night, hissing her from sleep. It hypnotized her with voices, spoke to her in the dark, silent hours, terrified her with what it might say. What it might make her do.

The thought of being pregnant, at first a weapon to use against her father, became a dread. She shrank from the thought of her body being invaded, swelling out of control. The days of the calendar were an ordeal, ended at last by the blessing of her period, usually such a nuisance, and a thankful rummaging in her drawer for tampons. She didn't tell Ross that he was off the hook; she hardly spoke to him again. After a few half-hearted efforts to find out what was wrong, he gave up and started going out with a girl from year ten. Suzanne, who now considered ponies to be childish toys, put Basil up for sale, avoiding Kirsty when she came to the yard to pack up her things. Graham stopped coming down to the stables, and Kirsty treated him with silent hostility, avoiding him as much as she could.

Then Jay announced he was leaving for the States, and she was on her own.

She sat at her father's desk, his screen-saver drawing her in to a mindless swirl of colours that filled her brain.

What am I going to do? What now?

Tat, she thought. The pub. Ross and the others.

She moved her hand on the mouse, and the screen-saver

was replaced by icons. Her father's desk-top. She clicked on his word-processing program and looked at the list of directories. There it was: *Damage*, his work in progress. Another click for *File Manager*; then *File – Delete*.

Delete Directory C:/ Damage?

Yes.

Yes to All?

Yes.

Under a pile of papers she found the tattered manilla folder labelled *The Damage Done*. She picked it up and took it to her room. Clutching it, she stood and looked at herself in the mirror: a pale, thin girl with worried eyes, a girl no one would ever look at twice, a girl who could easily blend into a crowd and disappear.

She slid back the door of her wardrobe. It was so rare for her to wear anything other than jeans or jodhpurs that she could hardly remember what other clothes were in there. She pulled out a short black skirt and a skimpy top, laying them on her bed to put on after her shower.

"Kirsty! Aren't you coming down?" Jay yelled up the stairs when she came out of the bathroom, wrapped in a towel.

"In a minute."

She got dressed, putting on black tights and clumpy-heeled shoes. Then, her hands shaking, she put on make-up, outlining her eyes in dark grey. She brushed and brushed her hair till it was alive with electricity. The girl in the mirror was a different creature now, a teenage girl dressed for a night out, slender, provocative, with hair falling over one eye. Pleased with her disguise, she put on a short cardigan over the crop-top, checked her purse for money, picked up her father's folder and went downstairs. Not through the kitchen, but out of the front door, stopping by the dustbin to shove *The Damage Done* right down to the bottom, covering it with rubbish, bits of cellophane and cardboard and hoover dust and the packaging from Jay's present.

No one was around in the yard. She got on her bike, straddling it awkwardly in her tight skirt, and rode away.

Opening the door of *The Rising Sun* was a test of courage. Inside, there was smoky air, thumping music, loud laughter: people, lots of them, people she didn't know. Kirsty closed her eyes, grasped the door handle and went in. It was like diving into a cold swimming pool: making up her mind, forcing herself to do it.

She saw Ross and Ollie at the bar, with their backs to her; Tatjana, by the dartboard, talking to a boy Kirsty didn't know. How strange it was: people choosing to come here to congregate in the smoke. She pushed her way through, and touched Tat's elbow.

"Hi. I decided to come after all."

Tatjana looked at Kirsty in amazement, taking in the clothes, the make-up. "What are you up to?"

"Nothing! Just felt like a night out with friends, that's all." Kirsty took out her purse. She looked across at the bar, where Ross stood waiting to be served, and caught his eye. He looked at her uncertainly, then smiled; she gave him a wide smile in return, and flicked back her hair.

"Get me a drink, will you?" she asked Tat, who could easily pass for eighteen. "I feel like getting smashed tonight. Vodka and tonic." It was the first thing she thought of. Having no idea what it would cost, she passed Tat a five-pound note.

"Kirsty!"

"Get one for yourself, if you want."

Tatjana shrugged, said, "This is Greg, by the way. Greg, Kirsty. D'you want something else?" she asked him.

Greg said, "No, I'm OK, thanks," and looked at Kirsty warily as Tatjana went up to the bar, leaving them together.

Kirsty felt exposed and conspicuous, the music thumping inside her head, the laughter jangling. She focused on Greg's face in an effort to stop herself from panicking. He looked older than Tatjana and herself, and had a long, serious face beneath tightly curled hair. "I haven't seen you before, have I?" she asked brightly.

"No, I'm a friend of Tat's. Staying with her for the weekend."

"How did you meet her?" Kirsty heard her voice making polite conversation, without a tremble, yet all her concentration was on standing upright, not letting herself be swayed by the maddening beat of the music. The air was stale, smoky, hard to breathe.

"At a sixth-form GM conference," Greg said.

"GM?"

"Genetic modification," Greg said, looking at her as if at a moron.

"Oh. Right." Aware of Ross looking at her from the bar, Kirsty gave him a sidelong glance and pushed her hair out of her eyes. He would come over and speak to her in a minute, and then she would –

The idea slid into her mind and stayed there, glinting, enticing. When Tatjana came back with the drinks, Kirsty downed hers quickly, then went over to Ross and tickled him from behind, making him wriggle and turn round. "Hi!" she said, and kissed his ear. He looked at her in some surprise, but caught her wrist and laughed.

"Hi, Kirsty," said Ollie. "Thought you'd gone into hiding or got married to a horse. Haven't seen you for months."

"No, I know," Kirsty said. "I'm making up for it now."

"You going on somewhere afterwards, or what?" Ross asked, looking at her clothes.

Kirsty leaned closer to him and whispered in his ear, "That depends."

"Oh yeah? On what?"

She giggled. "On you."

"See you later, you two. I'm beginning to feel a bit surplus to requirements." Ollie picked up his drink and moved away to join Ella.

Ross put his arm round Kirsty's waist. "I've missed you."

"What happened to that Year Ten girl?" she asked. "Lucy

or whatever her name was? Did you get fed up with cradle-snatching?"

"That all finished ages ago. I dumped her. She was OK, but she's not like you."

He was such a pushover. Kirsty looked at his neat, regular features, his flawless skin and well-cut hair; he smiled his I-know-I'm-gorgeous smile. Soon he bought her another drink, and offered her a cigarette; she smoked it, trying to look sexy as she narrowed her eyes and exhaled. The smoke burned her throat and made her eyes sting. It felt horrible, not the sort of thing you ought to do to yourself, but she persevered, to impress Ross. Finishing her drink, she asked him to buy her another. She was aware of glances from Tat and Ella and the others; she and Ross were an item again. She giggled and laughed and threw back her hair to make sure everyone noticed. Then she whispered to Ross, "Is there one of those machines in the men's loo?"

His eyes widened. "What, condoms, you mean?"

"Yes. Is there?"

"I think so. Never used it."

"Well, you can use it now. How much do you need?" She took out her purse.

"Two pounds, I think. You get a pack of two."

There were two pound coins in her purse; she gave them to him. "Here. Go and get some."

Ross looked at the coins in his hand, then grinned. "You think two's going to be enough?"

When he had gone, Kirsty went over to Tatjana and drew her away from the group. "If my Dad phones later, I'm spending the night at your place, OK? Just tell him I'm in the bath, or something, if he wants to speak to me."

"What are you *doing*?" Tat said, in a furious whisper. "You're drinking too much, you never usually smoke, you're throwing yourself at Ross – what's going on?"

"I can if I want to, can't I? What's it got to do with you?"

"You're my friend, and I don't like to see you making a fool of yourself," Tatjana hissed.

"Oh, lighten up! Just 'cos I don't want to have a debate about GM crops with you and Greg! You're the one who's always trying to get me to the pub – well, now I'm here, and you can't tell me what to do! I'm at your house if anyone asks, OK?"

"I'd prefer it if you left me out of this. Are you getting back at Adam or something?"

"Adam?" Kirsty remembered, just in time, who he was. "Oh, that. It's all finished."

"So now you're boomeranging back to Ross. Is that fair?"

"Fair to who?" Kirsty stared; Tatjana's face was blurring, becoming a talking mouth. What did fairness have to do with it? Dad wasn't fair, Jay wasn't fair: why should she be?

"To Ross, obviously. I just hope you know what you're doing –"

"Course I do! I'm not a little kid. Ross is getting some condoms this very minute."

"And that's all that matters, I suppose," Tatjana said, acidly.

"Yes, it is! You're doing it with Greg, aren't you? He's staying with you, he told me."

"That's different!"

"No, it's not. It's just that your parents don't mind. Remember. If my dad checks up, I'm staying with you."

The room was blobbed with faces. The swell of laughter and conversation rose and fell like waves. Seeing Ross come out of the Gents', Kirsty went back to him and sidled on to a bar stool.

"Got them?"

"In my pocket."

"Give them to me!" She held out her hand.

"What, now?"

"They're mine! I paid for them, didn't I? And I'm looking after them. Come on."

Surreptitiously, Ross reached into his pocket. "You going to show everyone?" He passed her the packet in a closed hand.

"Thanks." She put it into her bag, and smiled at him triumphantly.

She stayed with Ross, drinking and smoking, till last orders were called. Tatjana, leaving with Greg, looked at her disapprovingly. Ross leaned across to Kirsty and kissed her neck, and said, "I was going back to Ollie's. He's got his brother's car. Want to come? We can both stay, his parents are away. Ollie won't mind."

"Great," Kirsty said. "I've told my dad I'm staying at Tat's."

Boys are such idiots, she thought; you can do anything with them. At closing time, she went to the Ladies' loo, telling Ross she'd see him in the car park at the back. When she had finished, Kirsty went straight out of the front door into the cool night. She filled her lungs with air and looked up at the sky. A thousand stars hung there, pricking the blackness, making her feel dizzy. The moon was a sharp, clean crescent, a slice of light. The buzz of noise from the pub, like an angry wasp ricocheting against the sides of her head, faded into silence as she pushed her bike along the quiet street.

Not home. The other way.

She had to see Dally.

CHAPTER 17

There was only the sliver of moon to show her the way. She hauled her bike off the road and hid it in the bushes by the entrance to the track. Without the feeble beam of its headlight, darkness closed around her. She waited for her eyes to adjust, for the trees to arch overhead, showing starry sky through their branches. Stumbling, her head fuzzy with vodka, she picked her way along the path. On some nights she had seen the moon full and bright enough to cast moonshadows, had stayed out in the fields or yard to enjoy the weirdness of it. Not tonight. A faint wind stirred the trees; a branch near her creaked and creaked, like a sound effect for a Gothic ghost film. She shivered, wondering why she wasn't scared to walk here alone; more afraid that Dally wouldn't be in the cottage. He's got to be, she thought; if he's not, I'll just sit down and wait till morning. I'm not going home.

The cottage loomed beside her, a black square blocking off the sky. She went to the front door and looked inside, seeing candles, and the back door open. He must be here! But the door didn't yield to her pushing. The back way, then. Feeling her way by the fence, she came to the back gate and saw Dally sitting on the ground leaning against the cottage wall, with a candle in a saucer beside him.

"Dally! It's me!" she whispered.

Instantly he scrambled to his feet and turned to face her. When he spoke, his voice was husky, unsteady.

"*Kirsty!* God, you nearly gave me a heart attack!"

"Sorry." She slid the gate open and went in, tripping on the uneven grass. "What were you doing?"

"Nothing. Just sitting. What are *you* doing?"

"I had to see you. I had to." She went straight to him and put her arms round his thin body, resting her face on the rough wool of his sweater. His arms went round her, holding her.

"Why? What's happened?"

"My brother's going back to the States. He's getting married."

"You weren't expecting that?"

"No, he was going to come back, in September, and we had all sorts of plans for the yard, making it a proper training centre, and I know you don't like it, but it was going to be so great, and now he's going to leave me on my own and he thinks it doesn't matter – oh, I *hate* him, him and my dad! You *said* my dad was a shit, and you're right –" A choking sob rose in her throat. Dally said nothing, but stood stroking her hair, just as she had seen him stroke a horse.

"Dally," she said into his sweater. "Let me stay here with you. Please?"

He let go of her. "Where've you been? You smell like an ashtray." He sniffed. "What've you been drinking?"

"Only vodka. I went to the pub. I had to get out of the house. And my friend Tat's going to cover for me, say I'm with her. It's all right, she doesn't know anything about you. Please let me stay! Were you going to sleep out here?"

"No, it's much too cold. And you're shivering. I was looking at the stars. But I was about to turn in. It's not very luxurious here, you've seen it. But you can stay if you want. There's a spare horse-blanket, but you'll probably be cold." He went into the cottage and started rummaging about. The candles gave a flickering light, making shadows that reared and danced.

Didn't he understand? "Not if I sleep with you. Please, Dally. I want to." She followed him inside; when he turned, she put both arms round his neck and lifted her face to his in an awkward attempt at a kiss. For a moment she felt the warm press of his lips before he turned aside, pushing her arms away.

"It's OK, honestly – look!" She unfastened the bag slung across her shoulder, took out the pack of condoms and handed it to him. He took it, looked at it puzzled for a second, then shoved it back.

"*No.* No."

His anger was like a shower of cold water in her face. She stood trembling. Dally, ignoring her, took off his boots and socks, then his jeans and shirt, and got into his sleeping-bag.

"Why?" Kirsty asked, her voice wavering. "Why won't you? Is it that other girl?"

"What other girl?"

"You know. Your sculpture. Your clay girl." Kirsty looked round and saw the clay model against the wall where Dally had left it yesterday, with the horses. "You said you'd tell me."

"Yes, I did. Only not now. And it's nothing to do with her anyway." He lay down, wriggling himself into the quilted bag.

"Why, then?" Kirsty pleaded. "I thought you liked me, just a bit?"

"You're not using me to get back at someone else," Dally said curtly. "You can stay if you want, but not for that." He rolled over, so that all she could see of him was a hunched shoulder.

Kirsty sat on a crate and hunched forward, pressing her fists into her eyes. Hopelessness washed over her. What now? Outside there was the long rutted track, the dark night, the road home to two people she couldn't face. Here was Dally, who didn't want her. He made no movement, and she thought he had fallen asleep; then he turned, stretched out an arm and said, "Come here, stupid. You'll get cold."

He sat up and unzipped his sleeping bag along its length, spreading it out flat. "Come on," he repeated, as she hesitated. "You can't sit there shivering. I don't want you dying of hypothermia. Come and get warm. Only no messing about, OK?"

She kicked off her shoes and got under the sleeping bag beside him. He pulled her close, resting his chin against the top of her head, and lay still.

She was puzzled. "Don't you do sex, or what?"

"Not on demand, no," he said, his voice in her hair. "When you really want to, and when I really want to, then OK. But not now. And preferably when you don't stink like a used ashtray."

"Sorry. I'm sorry."

"You've got yourself in a right state," he said. But his body was warming her, his quietness taking away the tension that had gripped her head like tightening elastic.

"I can't go to places like pubs." Her voice was muffled under the sleeping bag. "Towns. Out. I can't go to places where there are people." She felt the slight turn of his head, listening. "I had to make myself. That's why I got in a state, why I got drunk. I can't do it otherwise."

He was silent for a moment, then he said: "I know."

"What do you mean, you know?" she retorted; then blankness was replaced by a tingle of recognition. "You're the same! You can't do it either – that's why you live here –"

"No," he said flatly. "That's not why. Crowds, tube trains, I don't specially like them, but they don't send me into a panic."

"Then how can you know?" Her voice was small with disappointment.

"I told you before, I know what it's like inside your head. You don't have to tell me. But you can tell me if you want."

"Yes, I could." But there was no need to, and maybe that was better. She let herself sink towards sleep, until a thought pushed itself forward for attention. "*When*. You said *when* just now, not *if*. Did you mean that?"

"I never say anything I don't mean," Dally said. "Don't you know that yet?"

She lay still. The floor was hard beneath the blankets, pressing against her hip, but she didn't move. Outside, an owl hooted, the only sound in the silence that wrapped the cottage and pressed against its windows. The candles flickered, burning down in their saucers, throwing the shadows of the clay girl and the clay horses large and eerily lifelike against the wall. But the stillness of night was different here, not threatening at all; the closeness of another body was more comforting than she could have imagined. She heard Dally's soft breathing as he slid into sleep.

"Kirsty. Wake up! It's morning. You've got to go."

She opened her eyes, blinked, remembered. Grey light filled the blank squares of window. Dally, already up and dressed, was crouching, his hand on her shoulder. When had he left her? How had she not noticed?

He bent to kiss her eyebrow. "Come on, ashtray. Time to get up."

She wanted him to kiss her properly, but not yet. Her throat was parched, last night's cigarette smoke foul in her mouth. When she raised herself on one elbow, the cottage reeled around her, then came slowly to rights.

"I want to stay here," she protested. "Why've I got to go?"

"You need to go home and sort things out. You can't hide here."

She saw that his hair was wet and roughly towelled. "You've been swimming!"

"I always do."

"Oh, why didn't you wake me up? I could have come too!" She imagined herself and Dally swimming naked in the dawn lake, surrounded by birdsong and rising mist, their hair streaming like weed, their limbs entwining underwater. It was a soft-focus vision that had little to do with actuality, the hard floor and her need to pee.

"You were fast asleep," Dally said. "Come on." He handed her the discarded cardigan. "I'll get you some water. You've got blodgy make-up all round your eyes."

Kirsty stood up and tugged at her skirt, feeling awkward and ridiculous in her pub clothes. She looked around for a non-existent mirror. "Oh, God. I must look a state."

"Yes, you do. I prefer you as yourself, not all dressed up," Dally said. "You look like any other tarty girl. I like Kirsty better." He poured water from a bottle into a mug, then dipped his fingers in and gently smoothed them over her eyelids and under her lower lashes. She watched his intent expression, his ugly-beautiful face that made her see other faces as bland, his eyes that she could now see were a light, clear grey. We slept together, she thought; he kissed me.

"That's a bit better," he said. "It won't come off properly though."

"I need a shower. And the loo. There isn't a bathroom here, is there?"

"I haven't got en-suite with fluffy towels and a jacuzzi, no. You can pee in the woods."

Kirsty put on her shoes and went outside, behind a clump of brambles. It felt very early, the first birdsong silvering the trees' canopy; the grass was soaking, the air cool against her face. When she came back, Dally was boiling water on his camping stove. She stared at him, aghast, remembering.

"Oh, God. I deleted Dad's work, off the hard disk. And I chucked his folder in the dustbin, his paper copy."

Dally looked up. "You did what?"

"Deleted it. His drama script. The whole directory. I can't go back – he'll kill me! Dally, what am I going to do?"

"It's not as drastic as all that, is it? If you put his folder in the dustbin, it's still there. And he probably keeps a back-up disk if he's got any sense. Even if he hasn't, you can usually retrieve stuff you've deleted. It's still there in the system."

"How do you know?" Kirsty couldn't put Dally and computers into the same thought.

He poured hot water into two mugs. "I haven't always been a hermit. I do know things."

Kirsty sat down on the spread sleeping-bag. "Where did you live before? Where do you come from? You say you never tell me anything that's not true, but that's because you never tell me anything at all. I want to know everything about you."

"No, you don't. Not everything." Dally handed her a mug of coffee. "Drink this, then go home and tell your dad what you've done. Serves him right."

She clasped her hands round the hot mug. "But there's Jay. Leaving."

"You can't stop him."

"No." Kirsty gazed at a candle in its saucer, a blackened stump in a pool of congealed wax.

"He calls you Mouse," Dally said. "Is that how he thinks of you? A small, bright-eyed, scampering creature? Or mouse as in mousy – shy, quiet?"

"Shy and quiet, I should think. It goes back to when we were kids. I don't mind it." She thought: I wasn't shy last night. Not shy enough. I came round here and practically threw myself at him. She felt ashamed, looking down at her skirt, her legs in black tights. She should know by now that Dally never did what she expected.

Dally didn't answer. He drank from his mug, then he

looked at her and said, "Come back later. Today. And as yourself. Not as a tart, not as a mouse. Come back as Kirsty."

The back door was unlocked. Kirsty went quietly through the kitchen and into the main room, intending to tiptoe quietly upstairs to her room.

Her father was sitting on the sofa, smoking, staring at the floor. A rumpled blanket was spread beside him.

"Kirsty!" He got to his feet and wrapped her in a bear hug. His unshaven face prickled against hers; she could smell coffee on his breath. "Where've you been?"

"I –"

"Jay told me – God, I've been so worried –" He pushed a hand through his hair, looked at her more closely. "Where did you go? Mouse, you haven't done anything stupid, have you?"

"No," Kirsty said. Going to Dally had been the only sensible thing to do.

"Sit down. Are you OK, you're really OK?"

Kirsty nodded, suddenly overwhelmed with tiredness. She sat; her father wrapped the blanket round her shoulders, as if she was suffering from shock. And then feet clumped down the stairs, and Jay was in the room, rumpled and tired, in a towelling bathrobe.

"Mouse, for Christ's sake! Where were you? Couldn't you have phoned?"

"No, I couldn't."

"Why not? Where the hell have you been? Didn't you think how worried we'd be?"

"Didn't *you* think?" Kirsty retorted.

"You weren't with Tatjana, you weren't with Ross – where *were* you?" Jay stood, arms folded, chin jutting.

"You've been checking up on me? What business is it of yours, where I go, who I'm with?"

"We just wanted to know you were safe," Graham said, his arm still round her.

"Actually," Kirsty said, facing Jay, "I was with Dally. I spent the night with him. We slept together."

"You *what*? Dally – who the hell's Dally?"

"You know! Mrs Hendy's gardener. We saw him the other day, at the shop."

"What, that – Mrs Hendy's *gardener* – Christ, what is this, *Lady Chatterley's Lover*? I just hope you had the sense to use a condom, that's all."

Kirsty felt her father's hand tighten on her shoulder. "Jay –" he warned.

"No. We didn't," Kirsty said.

Jay raised his eyes to the ceiling, then closed them and sighed heavily. "Oh, great. Fantastic. You've never heard of AIDS, I suppose? Or teenage pregnancy? Oh no. Can't happen to me. Is that what you think? What if you've got yourself pregnant? Have you thought how that'd mess up your life? *Christ*, you must be stupid – rushing after someone you hardly know, looking like a slapper. Haven't you got any self-respect?"

"Shut up! Shut *up*!" Kirsty struggled to her feet. "Don't make it sound sordid! It's all right for you, isn't it, you and Emma – it's all right for . . . for . . . everyone except me – you've all got someone, haven't you? Never mind Kirsty, she can stay here and do all the work, I'll just clear off and have a fantastic time in the States – that's how much *you* respect me, isn't it?" She turned to her father. "And you – you – how can you criticize? Oh, I hate you, both of you!"

She sat down again, heavily, a hard sob rising in her throat.

"Shh, shhh. It's all right, Kirsty." Her father cuddled her, rocked her like a small child. "I'm not criticizing. Jay, go and make us some tea, can you? I want a private talk with Kirsty."

Jay opened his mouth to say something, then changed his mind and shrugged. He went into the kitchen, closing the door behind him, and started to bang about.

"I don't want to hear any of your excuses!" Kirsty hissed at her father.

He shook his head. "I'm not making any. I'm sorry, Kirsty. Please believe me. Jay told me about going back to the States. I can't stop him, but I told him how terribly unfair he's being to you—"

"*He's* being unfair! What about—"

"I know, I know. I told you, I'm not making excuses. I'm not very proud of myself, believe me. I've taken you for granted, haven't I? I haven't given you enough time, I've been too wrapped up in myself and my work –"

Kirsty shuddered, thinking of her hand hovering over the mouse: *Delete Directory C:/ Damage?*

Click.

Months of work gone. Lost.

"Dad," she said. "I've done something really awful. Unforgivable."

"Tell me," her father said quietly.

"Last night," she began, and her voice blurred with tears. "I was so angry – with Jay, and then you – I—"

"'Scuse me, Dad." It was Jay, opening the door a crack. "Sorry to interrupt, but the police are here."

"Police? What on earth for?"

Kirsty's hand flew to her mouth. "The horses! Have you checked the horses?"

"Not yet. It's early." Jay opened the door wider and came into the room, followed by two policemen: the handsome blue-eyed one, and an older man Kirsty hadn't seen before. Graham stood up.

"Mr Millen?" Blue-eyes held out a hand and shook Graham's. "DC Schofield. Sorry to disturb you at this time of the morning –" his eyes flickered to Kirsty, taking in her tearfulness, her going-out clothes – "but you may be able to help us. We're looking for a young man called Ian Dallimore."

Kirsty's sharp intake of breath gave her away. DC Schofield looked at her. Too late, she tried to cover up.

"About the horse attacks? But I thought you had someone? Two boys, you said."

"We have arrested two boys, yes. But we'd like to have a little chat with Ian Dallimore. Do you know where he is?"

Kirsty looked back at him defiantly. "I don't know anyone called Ian."

"But you do know someone called Dally," Jay said.

"That's right. He's Mrs Hendy's gardener, at Ravenswood. Why don't you go and ask her?"

"Because he's not at Mrs Hendy's," the officer said. "And one of your clients, Miss Wilcox, told us she'd seen him here last week."

Thanks a lot, Alison, Kirsty thought.

"Kirsty, don't try to cover up." Jay gave her an exasperated look. "I've just told them you were with him last night."

Kirsty gave him a look of loathing. Everyone in the room was looking at her; the older officer wore an expression of wearied amusement, as if he'd seen this a hundred times before. Her father touched her arm.

"So, Miss Millen," DC Schofield asked, "where exactly did you spend the night? Can you tell us, please, in your own words?"

"Who else's words am I likely to use?"

Pleased with her smart retort, Kirsty glanced at her father and saw him suppressing a smile. The policeman's eyes narrowed in annoyance. "Answer the question, please."

"At his house," Kirsty said. "I can't remember exactly where it is, 'cos it was dark and I've never been there before. He lives in Wolverton –" What had he told her, so long ago?

"Near the station, I think. I'd had a lot to drink and I didn't really notice."

"Come on, Kirsty. We know that's not true. You didn't go to his house, did you? Young Mr Dallimore hasn't been at home for several weeks now and his parents would rather like to know where he is." DC Schofield looked at her sternly. "Now I think you'd better tell us the truth. Where did you go?"

"Tell him, Mouse," Jay said.

CHAPTER 18

Kirsty's first thought was that she must warn Dally. As soon as the police had gone, she was upstairs, changing into jeans and a shirt. Leaving Jay to see to the horses, she biked round to Ravenswood.

She intended to go straight to the cottage, but as she passed the main entrance she saw the police car there, parked on the gravel in front of the house.

Kirsty knew that DC Schofield hadn't believed her. Dally had met her outside the pub, she had said; they had spent the night in the woods.

"Oh, really?" he said, looking up from his notebook. "Hardly *Midsummer Night's Dream* weather, is it, this time of year?"

"Actually, since you ask, it was more like *Lady Chatterley's Lover,*" Kirsty said, darting a look at Jay; the older officer suppressed a laugh. "But if you want to talk to Dally, he works in the garden every day of the week. You've only got to go round and find him. Didn't Mrs Hendy tell you that? He hasn't got anything to hide. He'd never hurt a horse, or any other animal, if that's what you think."

DC Schofield looked at her. "It's nothing to do with the horses."

"Then what is it to do with?"

"That's something I'd prefer to discuss with Mr Dallimore himself," he said, snapping his notebook shut.

Now, she wondered whether it had been such a good idea to rush round. She was making it look as if Dally *did* have something to hide; and she couldn't go to the cottage, or she might unintentionally lead the police there. In an agony of indecision, she cycled back home. *Could* Dally have done something criminal? She no longer suspected him of harming the horses, but could he have stolen something? Was he into drugs? Why would he choose to live like a hermit, if not to run away from something he couldn't face?

Later. She would see him later. It made no difference, what he had or hadn't done.

The morning wore on, leaden and slow. Kirsty and Jay were curt with each other. Jay helped with the horses, rode out on Leo and cleaned his tack, avoiding her. "I thought Leo was *my* horse now?" Kirsty said pointedly when he came back. Jay didn't answer. He was going to London next day, to visit their mother and buy Emma's present; he made no further suggestion that Kirsty might go with him.

Preoccupied with the need to see Dally, Kirsty had forgotten that she still hadn't told her father about the deleted files. When she saw him coming down the path from the house, her stomach lurched unpleasantly – he's found out, she assumed, and was coming to yell at her. Then she saw that he was carrying a tray with three mugs of coffee on it and was smiling genially. He's still on his best behaviour, she thought: that'll change in a minute, when I tell him. But Jay came out of the tack-room and they all looked at Dorcas and the foal while they drank the coffee. Kirsty couldn't confess now, not with Jay listening. It would have to wait till she'd seen Dally.

At lunchtime she could hardly eat. She had been in a fever of frustration all day, her stomach curdling. She nibbled at a sandwich and put most of it in the bin when no one was looking. Then, when her father went upstairs to catch up on lost sleep and Jay to e-mail Emma, she cycled back through the village and past Ravenswood, to the track that led to the cottage. Hiding her bike exactly where she had put it last night, she ran down the path.

The cottage was empty. The front was locked up, but the back door yielded to her push and she stood on the threshold looking in dismay at the bare floor, at the place where Dally's belongings had been. Nearly everything had gone – his sleeping-bag, his camping stove, his rucksack. Only the horse-blankets and the crates were left, the blankets neatly folded. He had punctiliously taken only what belonged to him, leaving behind the things he had borrowed. Kirsty went inside and crouched on the floor where the makeshift bed had been, the place where she had slept with him last night. She touched the bare boards of the floor.

The model horses were still there, by the wall, in their various frozen attitudes. The goose, with Dally's fingermarks in the clay. Kirsty looked. All the models were there except one. The Ophelia girl. Dally wouldn't leave that one behind.

Her first thought was: did he go before or after the police found him?

And her second: how will I ever see him again?

She had to. Dally was her lifeline, her anchor. Without ever saying much, he had given her the reassurance she needed, answering panic with calmness, ditherings with bluntness, hysteria with simple truths. It didn't matter that she knew so little about him; he just was.

And now he was somewhere else.

Where? Had he found out in time and moved on? Or was he, at this very moment, shut up in a police cell, or being interrogated? If the police had found him here, he might think she had given him away, and that was the worst thought of all. She *had* betrayed him, with her stupid boast to Jay and her father.

His absence was a terrible blank, a black hole. I've taken him for granted, Kirsty thought, just as Dad's treated me. She had expected him always to be here, mowing the grass or weeding the borders, or sitting outside staring at the stars, quite content to be alone.

She sat on the floor and wept, till a moving blur in her vision distracted her and became a spider. Sniffing, hugging her knees, she watched its progress. The thought clicked into her mind that Mrs Hendy must know something. He must have given her an address, a phone number, when he answered her job advert. She wiped her eyes on her shirt-sleeve and got up.

Mrs Bishop was in the kitchen, scouring the sink with her sleeves rolled up and listening to the radio: "I've got a bone to pick with you, Tony Archer," someone was saying. She looked round as Kirsty came in.

"You're looking for Dally, I suppose?" she said sharply. "No good he turned out to be. We've had the police here this morning."

"I know," Kirsty said.

"Got himself into trouble of some sort. Drugs, I shouldn't wonder. I told Mrs Hendy she ought to be more careful about who she takes on."

But you liked him, Kirsty thought. You liked him more than I did, at first; why should one police visit change that?

"Actually it was Mrs Hendy I wanted to speak to," she said. "It's about – about my brother, Jay. She was keen to see him."

Mrs Bishop looked doubtful. "She often has an afternoon nap around this time. I'll see if she's come down yet."

She took a very long time. Someone on *The Archers* was complaining about New-Age travellers. Kirsty sat on the stool where Dally had sat eating toast; she smoothed a hand across the worn surface of the wooden table. A sponge cake was cooling on a wire rack; a small chicken was stuffed and trussed, ready for the oven. *I don't eat dead animals,* Dally had said. Everything kept coming back to him, to the blank of his absence.

Mrs Bishop's flat shoes clumped on the tiled corridor. "She'll see you. She's in the sitting-room. I'll bring some tea in a moment."

Mrs Hendy was sitting on one of her upright sofas – on rather than in, Kirsty thought, as the sofas seemed to offer little comfort. The old lady stood as she entered the room and extended her thin, reptilian hand.

"Sit down, Kirsty. I'm pleased you came to see me."

Oh? Kirsty looked at her in surprise. They both sat down, facing each other across the width of a Chinese carpet. Mrs Hendy, showing no sign of having recently slept, was neat in a cardigan-style suit and ruffled blouse, her feet precisely aligned in brown court shoes. Didn't she ever slop about in slippers like anyone else, Kirsty wondered?

"I imagine you've come to ask me about Dally," Mrs Hendy said.

"Well – yes."

"He's gone, you know that?"

"I –" Kirsty gazed back, thrown, unable to read the old lady's expression. She didn't look tight and disapproving like Mrs Bishop – she looked, Kirsty thought, almost pleased. "Do you mean the police took him away? Mrs Bishop told me they'd been."

"No. Not the police. I didn't tell them Dally was living in the cottage."

Kirsty opened her mouth, closed it again, swallowed. "You *knew*?"

"Of course. I keep my ears and eyes open."

"And you don't mind?"

"No, why should I? It's sat empty for long enough. I'd have had the water and electricity turned on if he'd asked – I was waiting to see if he would. To be quite honest I liked having someone around the place at night. Even if he didn't know I knew."

"He thought you'd throw him out." Kirsty traced a swirl of pattern on the carpet with her toe.

"Yes, I know. I'm quite aware that he must have seen me as a crusty old woman living in far more luxury than anyone has a right to. I don't expect him or anyone else to approve. But the fact is that he interested me."

Kirsty looked up. Mrs Hendy's thin lips were pressed into a tight, knowing smile.

"I like people with individuality," the old lady said. "Strength of character. People who aren't afraid to do things their own way."

"You told Dally the police were looking for him?" Kirsty guessed.

Mrs Hendy nodded, pleased with her secret. "Yes. I told them he wasn't working here today, then I went to the cottage and told him. He decided to move on before they came back for him. It seems I'll be needing another gardener. I must put an advertisement in the paper."

Kirsty's mouth was dry. "Why do they want him? What's he done?"

And then Mrs Bishop came in with the tray of tea, and Kirsty sat bursting with tension while she unloaded a quite unnecessary amount of crockery on to a glass-topped table. There were doilies, and dainty cakes on a plate. Kirsty felt sick.

"Dally didn't quite tell me the truth, you know," Mrs Hendy said quietly when at last the housekeeper had gone out. "He lied about his age – told me he was twenty. And he gave me a false name. Dalloway, he called himself. I didn't check, didn't bother with references. I could tell I was going to like him."

He never lied to me, Kirsty thought. Even if he never said his real name was Ian. Then: stop thinking of him in the past tense! I must find him; Mrs Hendy must know *something* –

"So how old is he really?" she asked.

"Only seventeen. That's why the police want him. He's run away from home and his parents want him back."

"Why did you help him get away?"

"I thought he must have his reasons for leaving home."

"Isn't that aiding and abetting, or something?" Kirsty asked. "Not telling the police what you know?"

The old lady gave a slow smile that was almost mischievous. "Yes, I'm sure it is. But at my age, what have I got to lose?"

"I've got to find out where he is," Kirsty said flatly.

"I can't help you with that, because I don't know. But he gave me something for you." Mrs Hendy got stiffly to her feet and went out to the hallway. Kirsty's eyes followed her, willing her to hurry. A message? An address? But when Mrs Hendy came back, she held a round object cupped in her hand. She gave it to Kirsty. It was a clay model of a cat – a tiny, curled, sleeping cat. Perfect. Freda, Kirsty thought.

"Did he say anything?" Kirsty asked, searching the old lady's face.

"No. Just 'Give this to Kirsty.'"

"No message? Nothing?"

"Just the cat. I'm sorry." Mrs Hendy looked at her. "If he wants to contact you, then I'm sure he knows how to."

If. Kirsty couldn't think about that *if.* She knew who was more important to Dally – the sad girl, the girl he had modelled. The only clay model he had taken away with him. Where else would he go, but to find the Ophelia girl?

At home, between the stableyard and the house, she stopped at the dustbin and rummaged for the manilla folder. She brushed away the dust and fluff, and went to see if her father was awake.

"Dad?"

"Mmm?" he answered, from his bedroom.

Kirsty went in. She had never been into that room, not

once, since the incident with Suzanne. When she hoovered and dusted upstairs, she left Graham to do his bedroom and study himself, though he rarely bothered. When it had been her mother's room too, it had been neat and feminine, smelling of perfume. Now the dressing-table had acquired a layer of clutter, of books, papers, letters. The chair was heaped with discarded clothes, in the midst of which slept Nutmeg, peacefully curled.

"Dad? Haven't you been working this morning?"

Graham yawned and sat up. "Not really. A few letters and phone calls, that's all. Why?"

Kirsty clutched the folder. "Because I did something awful. You know I started to tell you –"

He looked at her. "Go on. Tell me now."

"I deleted your work," Kirsty said. "All of it. Your *Damage Done*. And I threw this in the bin. But here it is."

She held it out to him. He took it, turned it over, slid out the wad of papers from inside.

"You deleted it?" he said blankly. "My whole directory? All the work I've been doing for the last few months?"

"Yes."

Her father said nothing. He swung his feet to the floor, put on his shoes and laced them. Then he went through to his study and plugged in the computer. Kirsty followed him. He sat on his office chair and waited for the load-up process; then he clicked the mouse a few times, searching, and swivelled round to face her.

"Yes, you have. Why?"

He was speaking quite calmly. She waited for the flash of anger.

"I wanted to hurt you," Kirsty said, pushing the words out past a lump in her throat. "To get my own back."

He nodded slowly. "Yes."

"What do you mean, yes?"

"I mean yes, of course you did. I don't blame you. If you really had lost all my work, it'd probably serve me right."

"It's not lost, then?"

"No, I've got my back-up." He pulled out a disk from the plastic box on the desk. "I always copy, at least once a day. I'm disorganized about most things, but not with that. I can copy straight back. Here it is, *The Damage Done.*" He smiled, sadly. "The damage undone. That part, anyway."

"What?"

"Come here, Mouse." He held out his arms to her; she went to him, and he pulled her to stand close beside him.

"I thought you'd be furious!" she said to the top of his head.

"I am furious. With myself. And a bit with Jay. We started having this conversation this morning, didn't we? Let's finish it now."

"What are we talking about?"

"About us. You and me, living here, getting along together. Because there's just the two us of now, and we've got to do

224

better than we have done. *I've* got to do better." He twisted round, looking up at her. "I've been too wrapped up in my work, I know that. Too selfish, is what it comes down to. I haven't taken enough notice of you. Haven't given you enough help. I've been writing about the damage people do to themselves with drugs – turning a blind eye to the simple damage one person can do to another, by ignoring them, by taking them for granted. I'm sorry. Really sorry. I'm going to do a lot better, Mouse, from now on. I'll give you any help you need." When she didn't answer, he gave her a little shake and said, "I mean it. Don't you believe me?"

"I suppose so."

"We're going to make it work, aren't we? We've got to." He leaned the side of his face against her arm. "You gave me such a fright last night, when you disappeared. I thought you'd left home, run off for ever, and I wouldn't have blamed you."

They were both silent. From the muddy swirl of Kirsty's thoughts one idea was clear; that she felt almost deprived of yesterday's urge to make a scene, to throw a tantrum. Then, she could justifiably have blamed everyone in the family for letting her down; now, with her father so contrite and so reasonable, she couldn't really think that any more. She would have known how to react if he'd been angry, the ammunition of her retorts all loaded and ready. She didn't know how to respond to this. It left her flat, deflated.

Graham said quietly, "I've lost Ursula, and now Jay. You're all I've got left, Mouse. I'm not letting you get lost as well."

CHAPTER 19

"Tat," Kirsty said, on the phone. "I was an idiot last night, and I'm sorry. And I lied to you."

"No, really?" Tatjana said drily. "What about?"

"About Adam. You know I told you it was all over? Well – I never went out with him at all. I don't really know why I told you I did."

Tatjana digested this, then said: "So what sent you spinning out of orbit last night, then?"

"Family trouble," Kirsty said. Putting it mildly. She added, "But there was someone. Someone else. And now he's gone and I'm really gutted about it."

"For God's sake *tell* me, next time," Tatjana huffed. "Better than taking it out on Ross, hurling yourself at him, then leaving him in the car park."

"He told you?" Kirsty was unable to suppress a giggle.

"Ollie did. Who's this someone else, then?"

"It doesn't matter. He's gone now."

"Well, don't put your life on hold," Tatjana said. "Just for some guy."

Kirsty thought about this afterwards. She would have taken Tatjana's advice on many things, but not this. Dally didn't come into any recognizable category; he wasn't just *some guy*. If I want to put my life on hold, Kirsty thought obstinately, then I will. Because on hold is where it is. If I want to be miserable, then I'm really going to wallow. I'm not going to pretend it doesn't matter, when it does.

To Jay and her father, she did pretend. Jay would think she was miserable because he was leaving and she didn't want to give him that satisfaction; and she wanted to go along with her father's idea that everything was fine now that they'd had their little chat. But to pretend to herself: that would have been dishonest. Whatever life offered had to be experienced to the full. To trivialize would be to cheat herself.

She looked up Dallimore in the telephone directory under the hall table. There was only one. *Dallimore, R. B. – Ryecote Lodge, Westland Road, Wolverton.*

Westland Road was the main street, the one that ran past the station and on to join the bypass. That must be it – R. B. Dallimore, Dally's father. The father who was trying to get him back.

That afternoon she cycled there. What she planned to do when she arrived, she had no idea; but she had to glimpse what Dally had run away from. As far as the station, Westland Road was lined with terraced houses with numbers; but the directory had given no number for Dally's house. Beyond the river bridge was a small park, a health centre, then big detached houses, each fronted by trees and well set-back from the road. There were elegant gardens, extensions, immaculate driveways. This didn't seem right. Kirsty didn't know what she had imagined for Dally's home, but not this kind of affluence. She must have made a mistake; Ryecote Lodge could, perhaps, have been one of the brick terraces –

But no, here it was. Set behind a screen of silver birches and hollies. Ryecote Lodge. A wide gateway, with the name on a black metal plaque. A big stone house with bay windows on either side of the porch; flanked by shrubberies, with a wrought-iron gate leading through to the back. The box of a burglar-alarm system was prominent under the eaves. There was a detached double garage, and ample parking space in front; Kirsty saw an Audi and a Land Cruiser. Everything about Ryecote Lodge spoke of wealth and security.

Kirsty leaned her bike against the wall, opened the gate and went in. She stepped into the porch, rang the bell. With no idea what to say, she waited for footsteps to approach from what seemed a long way off, a shadow to cross the glass of the front door. She had to see who lived here.

For a wild second she thought it might be Dally himself who opened the door. Then a woman stood there, gazing at her hopefully.

"I'm looking for my dog," Kirsty bluffed. "I was walking him in the park and he ran off."

Disappointment tugged at the woman's face, resignation

made her shoulders droop. Kirsty knew at once that this must be Dally's mother. And that Dally hadn't come home.

"No, I haven't seen a dog," the woman said. "But I don't suppose I would have taken much notice. What does he look like?" she added, without interest.

Kirsty made up some details. She studied the woman. There was no obvious resemblance – only a sort of wary, darting look that suddenly became Dally. Her eyes were lined and tired, indeterminate grey, just like his. This woman had well-cut greying hair and a made-up face and lipstick; she wore a cream sweater and black trousers and small gold earrings. She had lost her son, but still took the trouble to turn herself out carefully.

"How will I let you know if I do see him?" Dally's mother asked, when Kirsty had finished her improvisation.

"There's a poster on all the lamp-posts. It's got my phone number on it," Kirsty said.

"I hope you find him," Mrs Dallimore said dully, and closed the door.

Kirsty went back to her bike, shutting the double gates behind her. She looked back at the house. Ian Dallimore lived here. Ian Dallimore must have gone through these gates a thousand times, greeted his mum, slung his school bag on the floor and told her about his day. Ian Dallimore, who lived at Ryecote Lodge, was getting in the way of Dally. Kirsty could no longer quite remember what Dally looked like.

But later, when she lay in bed and looked at her model cat, she could remember. She had put it on her bedside table where she could see it at eye level. She could think of Dally's hands shaping it, his eyes focused; she could see his fierce concentration.

He had come and he had gone. That was all. The cat was his way of saying goodbye.

Moth lay on the duvet propped against the hump of Kirsty's feet, washing his face with great thoroughness. He licked a front paw and rubbed it against the side of his face, his eyes closed to slits; then, with a purring sigh, he settled to sleep. Kirsty envied him his perfect, smug contentment. It would be so easy to be a cat; completely happy with the moment, a full stomach, company, a warm bed to lie on. Why did being human mean wanting more than that?

She couldn't see beyond the black hole of Dally's absence.

Jay went back to the States at the end of the week. Kirsty was amazed at how little she minded, having readjusted her ideas about him so comprehensively. Now it was just Dad and her. And Lottie.

"I've been thinking," Lottie said, leaning on the paddock gate with Kirsty one evening. "With Dad so ill and everything, I'm giving up the idea of being a chalet girl. I probably wouldn't have liked it anyway."

Kirsty had a headcollar in her hand, to bring Leo in. Soon, she thought, as soon as the nights were reliably warmer, she would leave him turned out at night; now that the horse attackers had been caught, she could stop worrying. He was her horse now, and she could decide. "So what will you do instead?" she asked Lottie.

"I thought I might work here with you," Lottie said.

"*Really*? Why?"

"I like it here," Lottie said simply.

"My mum says it's just drudgery, mucking out stables."

"I like drudgery." Lottie waved a hand. "I mean, who'd go and work in some stuffy office when they could be out here, with all this?" She waved a hand to encompass Leo, the green swathe of paddock, the arrow-swoop of an early house-martin.

"Mum wants me to live in Putney and do a business studies course," Kirsty said.

Lottie stared. "You're not going to, are you? You'd be mad, when you can live here. And now you've got Leo, as well. What would you do with him in Putney?"

"It's OK, I'm not going. And it'd be great if you worked here, but how? There's no *money*. We only make what the liveries pay us, and that's not much. Are you going to drudge for nothing?"

"You can expand, can't you? That's what you and Jay were planning to do. You still can. And I thought I might get proper qualifications, for giving lessons – I mean, I've done a lot of teaching for the Pony Club, and done C test. It's not that much more difficult. Maybe in a year or two. . . Then we could buy a few ponies, set up as a proper riding school. It'd be fun, wouldn't it? And I could breed Welsh cobs," Lottie added wistfully.

"Oh yes? And where's the money coming from, for all that? My dad writes a world-beating best-seller, I suppose, or wins an Oscar for best screenplay? Are you sure you don't want an indoor arena and a cross-country course while you're at it?"

"Just an idea." Lottie pulled her pony-tail over her shoulder to disentangle bits of hay from its strands. "I thought you'd like the company. Forget it, if you think it's so stupid."

"Sorry," Kirsty said. "And thanks, if you really mean it."

She called Leo, who raised his head from grazing and walked unhurriedly towards her, his hooves brushing the grass. She walked to meet him; Lottie waited by the gate.

"You can enter Leo for Badminton and Blenheim," Lottie called to her.

"Oh, right. And win first time, obviously," Kirsty teased. "And be selected for the Olympic team and come back as a gold medallist. Easy."

Kirsty led Leo into his stable, where his feed was ready in the manger. She patted him, and stood admiring him, her horse. She leaned her face against his neck to breathe in his warm horse smell. Eating, he raised his tail and produced a series of neat round droppings that plopped on to the clean straw.

"If you're so keen to start drudging," Kirsty said to Lottie, who was leaning on the half-door, "there's a wheelbarrow and a shovel round the corner."

Kirsty kept thinking about the boy who lived at Ryecote Lodge. Ian Dallimore. Not really Dally. She imagined Ian Dallimore getting out of the Land Cruiser, going up to his spacious bedroom, turning on the stereo. Doing his homework, revising for exams. If he was only seventeen, he would have been in Kirsty's year at school, but she had never seen him.

She couldn't begin to see Dally in that environment. She could only see him by the stables, the lake, the cottage, in the hermit existence he had chosen.

Where was he now? There was nothing to keep him in this area. With the police after him, he'd be mad to stay. He could be a hermit anywhere he chose.

"Post," said Graham, who was expecting the fee for his writers' course. "I'll get it."

He came back into the kitchen sorting envelopes. "Boring . . . boring. . ." He chucked the gas bill and a bank statement on the kitchen table. "Oh, and one for you."

Kirsty never got much post. She took the envelope from her father, expecting something conciliatory from Jay. There was a postcard inside – a painting, four trees in a line, against a turbulent sky. She flipped it over and read the brief lines of handwriting.

"Kirsty, Meet me in Sounds Unlimited, Saturday, 2.30. Dally."

Her heart thumped. She read it again and again. The writing was difficult to read – large, elongated, with long swirling tails to the ys. His name and her name both ended with that same looping flourish. She had never seen his handwriting before. It suited him.

He hadn't forgotten her. And presumably he was still in the area – Sounds Unlimited was a small, independent music shop in the mall in Newington. She turned the card over again. Why would he choose a place like that?

"Anything interesting?" Graham asked. And then, turning back to his own mail, "Would you believe it – they've rejected my short story. And still no bloody course fee! I'm going to get on the phone." He looked at his watch. "Any chance of more coffee?"

Kirsty got up to make it. When her father had gone, still grumbling, up to his study, she looked again at her postcard. *Egon Schiele*, was the caption. *Vier Baume, 1917*: four trees against a stylized background of green hills. Three had foliage, bronze autumn leaves; the fourth was bare. Behind them, in the dip between hills, a craggy mountain ridge, and a red sun setting. Kirsty looked and looked, trying to read some significance into Dally's choice of image. A sun setting, autumn: the end of something? Or had he just liked the picture?

Saturday. Three days away.

CHAPTER 20

It was months since Kirsty had been into the town centre. Going on a weekday would be bad enough; to go on a Saturday was almost unthinkable.

Dally, in the shopping mall, in Sounds Unlimited? It seemed the most unlikely place for him to choose; even more incongruous than Ryecote Lodge. By Friday evening she had begun to wonder if it was a trick, set up by the police, or by Dally's mother.

But she had to go. She finished her yard jobs, went indoors to tidy herself up and put on a clean shirt, then made an excuse to her father about meeting Tatjana. She cycled the six miles to Newington, into the Saturday traffic. She left her bike padlocked to a stand by the war memorial and began her walk along the congested pavement.

There were people with baby buggies and bags full of shopping; there were groups of teenagers that took up the whole pavement. Buses passed so close that they almost brushed her arm; people came out of shop doorways without looking and bumped into her without apologizing. She smelled car fumes, hamburgers; her vision blurred with bustle and activity. It was her personal hell. Didn't Dally know that? She'd *told* him. Besides, he claimed to be able to get inside her head. If he were in there now, he'd want to get out again fast. Panic was a black swirl, a tightening band round her forehead, a thumping in her chest. Her throat was a repressed scream. If she let it out, she'd wake up and find herself alone in bed in the dark. If she let herself run, she would soon be back in green fields.

She made herself walk. One, two, one, two, her rhythm disrupted by people in her way, by a stupid boy who leaped out in front of her and pulled a leering face. The high street stretched out interminably, a jumble of coloured signs and moving humanity and screaming posters. With every step, she was further away from her bike, and home.

She pushed through glass swing doors into the shopping mall. Space and air enclosed her; glass panels soared above, letting in sky. The traffic noise was replaced by the steady tread of feet on tiled floor, the *clop clop* of high heels. She could walk more easily here. She fixed her gaze on the turn at the far end of the mall; Sounds Unlimited was there, past River Island and Tie Rack, Dixons and Dolcis. Ranks of summer shoes marched towards her, ties and knickers thrust themselves at the window glass. Stereos, Walkmans, a whole bank of TV screens all garish with the same picture that drew Kirsty's eyes irresistibly: identical cricketers in formation against brilliant green that hurt her eyes. The screens blurred, became a shrieking dazzle.

Sickness was shoving her stomach up towards her throat.

She was going to heave. She looked around desperately; where was the nearest toilet? Would she make it? She swallowed, tried to take regular, deep breaths. She closed her eyes and summoned her mantra, her image of the smooth lawn at Ravenswood, the quiet lake, the willows. If she fixed that image in her mind she could carry on walking, gulping down the sickness. Walk. One, two, one, two. It was like pushing against a current that forced her back. Her own body was fighting her, protesting, making itself heavy and sluggish.

But now here was Sounds Unlimited. A window display of grimacing faces; a heavy, repetitive beat pulsing out of the open doorway. Kirsty hesitated, looking at her watch. Two twenty. Dally didn't wear a watch; he never knew what the time was. Was he really going to turn up, here of all places?

Slowly she went inside. There were film posters, shelves of videos; people flicked through racks of CDs. Kirsty looked around wildly, her head full of the maddening electronic beat. No Dally. Her eyes were drawn to a beautiful dark-skinned boy behind the cash desk, serving a customer. He handed over change and receipt, and gave a dazzling smile; then he looked at Kirsty.

"Looking for anything special?" he asked her.

"Yes." Her voice came out far too loud. "I'm supposed to be meeting someone. But he isn't here."

"Oh, you mean Dally?" The boy turned and yelled through an open doorway behind him, "Dally! You're wanted!"

Feet clumped up a staircase and then suddenly there was Dally behind the cash desk. He looked at Kirsty without smiling, without speaking. His hair was tidy, cut shorter, and he wore a clean white shirt. The thudding in her chest became a tug of disappointment; he had turned ordinary. He was Ian Dallimore.

"Here I am," she said.

He nodded, unsurprised. "I was just unpacking some new stuff downstairs."

"You *work* here?"

"Yes. Karim's brother's the manager. I used to help out on Saturdays and now I'm filling in for a bit."

"Is this the normal life you said you might get back to?" Kirsty asked, thinking of Ryecote Lodge, and the sad-eyed woman.

"Not exactly," Dally said. "As normal as it's likely to get." The Asian boy was watching with interest; Dally noticed, and said, "Karim, this is Kirsty. OK if I go out for an hour?"

Karim nodded and smiled. Dally pulled on his old black jacket and said to Kirsty, "Come on. There's a place near here where we can get coffee."

I thought – I wanted – I didn't know – all jostled for a place on Kirsty's tongue, but she said nothing as she walked beside Dally through the crowded mall. He looked at her once and smiled, but said no more; he led the way out of the nearest glass door and down a narrow side-street. Kirsty, who had expected McDonald's or Pizza Hut, followed him into a small, tatty café with checked plastic tablecloths. A door-bell jangled; the air inside smelled of coffee and bacon. Two large men sat side by side at the table nearest the counter, elbows well out, eating great platefuls of egg, bacon and tomatoes. At the counter, a fat man with a tea-towel apron waved at Dally, who said, "Hi, Stan," and to Kirsty, "Coffee?"

Kirsty nodded, and Dally ordered two cappuccinos. The aproned man got to work at a many-spouted machine. "I'll bring them over," he told Dally, sliding his change across the counter. Dally led the way to a table at the back of the room. There was a vase with one plastic flower in it, salt and pepper in plastic pots and a bottle of tomato sauce; a dog-eared cardboard menu, propped up between them, was headed *Chez Stan*.

"I didn't even know this place existed!" Kirsty said, sitting down.

Dally sat opposite her. "I like it. It's where the market-traders come, and the lorry-drivers. Thought you'd prefer it to McDonald's."

"I do," Kirsty said. There was no loud music in here, there was space. She smiled at Dally.

"Most girls," he said, "would have turned up a bit late. A quarter to three, three o'clock. Just to show it's not that big a deal. You came early."

"It *is* a big deal," Kirsty said. "And I'm not most girls."

"No, you're not."

"I thought you never bothered with time?"

"When I'm working I have to," Dally said, and pushed back his left sleeve to show her a watch on his wrist. A sturdy, expensive-looking one, with several different dials. She thought of Ryecote Lodge, of Ian Dallimore who was wanted by the police. There were too many questions.

"Why did you make me come into town?" she asked him. "You know I hate it. It's my version of hell."

"It was a kind of test," Dally said, looking at her from under his eyebrows.

"Was it? Have I passed?"

He nodded. "You've done it, haven't you? You came. You've proved it to yourself. Proved you can do it if you want to. Now you can do it again."

"But I don't want to do it again." Kirsty fiddled with the edge of the menu, and read: *Stan's Scrumptious Snacks: Fill that gap with a doorstop bap.*

"You might. Once you know you can."

"Aren't you going to *tell* me anything?" Kirsty burst out. "I've gone through this awful struggle to get here – and you *knew* what it would be like – and now you're going to sit here talking in riddles as usual?"

Stan walked up slowly, whistling, with the two cups of coffee. He grinned at Dally, at Kirsty, placing the cups down carefully. The little finger of his right hand was missing; there was just a fat pink stump. Kirsty stared at it, then tried not to. "How's things then?" Stan asked Dally, propping himself against the edge of the table, settling for a chat. Kirsty's heart sank. Dally's hour would be up at this rate and she would know no more than she did already.

"Fine, thanks," Dally said. And then the door-bell jangled and an old man in a raincoat came in and stood inside the doorway, looking puzzled. Stan went back to the counter.

Kirsty leaned forward. "*Now* tell me! Please tell me! Why are the police looking for you? Where are you living?"

"OK," Dally said, smiling at her impatience. He ate the sugared biscuit that had come with the cappuccino. Then he said, "I was going to tell you about the clay girl. The model you saw."

"The one you took with you? The Ophelia girl?"

Kirsty's insides sagged with disillusionment. She thought: he's going to tell me he ran away to be with that girl. He's living with her now. That beautiful, elegant girl. Why's he bothering with me? It's not *fair* –

"Not Ophelia," Dally said. "Marianne. My sister."

"Your sister? I thought –"

"Yeah, I know. But she was my sister."

"Was?"

"Was. She was three years older than me. We didn't really get on all that well while she was at home, we were always squabbling and arguing like most people do, but – well. She used to play the violin – she wanted to be a professional musician, in an orchestra. I used to hear her practising in her room. Sometimes I'd go in and watch her and listen. I'd pretend to be looking through her books or her CDs, but really I was listening. She was good, but not good enough. She told me that, though she always sounded pretty brilliant to me. Her ambition was to be a soloist, to play the Beethoven Violin Concerto. She used to play it on CD in her room, all the different versions – Kennedy, and Ann-Sophie Mutter, and the Chinese one. . ."

"What happened to her?"

"Our parents." Dally's voice became hard-edged. "They didn't see that she'd ever have any sort of career as a musician. They pushed her and pushed her. She had to be an academic success. She'd be letting them down otherwise. She worked and worked for her A-levels till she nearly had a breakdown. She gave up playing her violin, she was studying every minute there was. She got her three As, though it nearly killed her. She got a place at Oxford. But that only made it worse."

"Why?" Kirsty said, starting to guess.

"Because she was convinced she'd be a failure. At school, OK, she was one of the brightest. She did it by hard grind, but she could do it. At Oxford, well *every*one was brilliant. Marianne knew she'd work her socks off and still there'd be people better than her. And if she failed –"

"Did she?"

"She couldn't get to the point of finding out. She drowned herself in the River Cherwell, halfway through her second year."

He gave Kirsty a pleading look, as if she might deny it. Her mouth opened in a soundless O.

"And I knew why," he went on. "She told me. She used to

tell me everything. In the holidays, she'd come home and pretend everything was great, to our parents. She was having a fantastic time, she told them – great friends, great tutors, good marks. And then she'd go up to her room and play the Beethoven Violin Concerto on her stereo, and cry. And she'd tell me, *I can't do it, Ian, I just can't do it.*"

"What did you do? Say?"

Dally looked at her. "All the wrong things. I told her of course she could, she'd done brilliantly in her A-levels, hadn't she? She'd be fine. What I should have done was tell Mum and Dad to lay off, stop expecting so much. Let her play her violin and have a good time being a student. Did it really matter a flying fuck what kind of degree she finished up with, as long as she was alive and happy? She couldn't see past it – what sort of return our parents would get for their investment. She walked down to the river that night thinking she was a complete and utter failure."

Dally looked at his coffee cup, picked it up and drank; Kirsty heard him swallow effortfully. She saw his eyes shiny with tears.

"Ophelia," she whispered. "She *was* Ophelia."

"Yes." He put the cup down. "How cold the water must have been, in February, how icy cold. I keep thinking that. As if it makes any difference. As if warm water would be nicer to drown yourself in."

"It wasn't your fault," Kirsty whispered, not knowing what else to say.

"I know. It was their fault. Our parents. They killed her. They killed Marianne."

"No." Kirsty wanted to reach for his hand across the table, but didn't; he would only shrug her off.

"They did. And they didn't even realize it. They blamed everyone else – her tutors, the college, even her friends – everyone except themselves. They didn't realize they'd done it to her."

"They didn't mean to."

"Maybe not – they did it all the same. They couldn't let her just *be*. They had to make her into something they wanted, something for themselves. And she let them, that was the terrible thing. She was going to be a lawyer, because that's what my dad is, because she would have failed otherwise. *You've got the ability, you've got all the advantages*, that's what they said to her. Even the music – she couldn't just play it and enjoy it, they had to put her through all the tests. As soon as she'd passed grade five, they'd start talking about grade six, then seven, eight – whatever she did, it wasn't enough. There was always another hurdle, another test she'd have to pass or fail. They've got enough money to give her everything, and they did – clothes, skiing holidays, a horse of her own – they were putting her through university. They gave her everything except what she needed. She was the girl who had everything, that's what the papers said when she died. Looks, brains, boyfriends, a plushy home, a bright future. She had everything except any sort of belief in herself. *It's like walking a tightrope* – that's what she told me. *I keep taking steps, struggling to keep my balance, but I'll always be wobbling and looking down to see how far I'll fall. And one day I will.* That's what she said."

"You must have thought about her," Kirsty said, "every time you swam in the lake. Is that why –?"

Dally didn't answer. He drank more coffee, put his cup down and touched the corners of his eyes.

"She was buried," he said. "They put her in the ground. In the earth. Marianne. Can you imagine that, Kirsty? Someone you love, being put in the ground to stay there for ever?"

"No," Kirsty whispered.

There seemed no more to say. She looked down at her own living hand, skin, knuckles, nails, and imagined Marianne's skilled, violin-playing fingers lying limp in a coffin. She looked across at Dally, not knowing what to do if he really broke down in tears. Being Dally, he probably would if he felt like it.

"I'm not going to be buried," Dally said. "Cremation's better. Still horrible, but done, finished. They're not putting me in the ground."

"Did they try to push you the same way, your parents?" Kirsty tried. "Is that why you left?"

He snatched a paper napkin from the metal holder and blew his nose on it, then stuffed it in his jeans pocket. "You're a bit like her," he said. "I don't mean in looks. I mean you're on the tightrope. You're putting on an act."

246

"Not with you, I'm not," Kirsty said. "With everyone else, but not you. You don't let me. What about you? Are you up there as well, on the high wire?"

"No," Dally said. "I'm not playing. I've packed my bags and said goodbye to the circus. D'you know that old kids' song about Nellie the Elephant?"

"I haven't got a clue what you're on about."

He hummed a snatch, tapping the rhythm on the table with his spoon. Then he stopped and looked at her seriously. "You can get help," he said. "You think you're all on your own, but you needn't be. I mean, once you stop keeping it all to yourself, you find out lots of people are like this. A doctor would know exactly what you're talking about. There are symptoms, just like there are for measles or flu. There are ways of making it better."

"How do you know?"

"I read books. I found things out. I talked to Marianne's best friend at Oxford, her flat-mate. All too late to be any use to her –" Dally's voice wavered; he bit his lip, looked away. "She used to have panic attacks, she'd wake up in the middle of the night and be terrified of nothing, she'd imagine hearing voices in her head. If only she'd gone to a doctor or a counsellor she'd have found out it wasn't really all that peculiar. It's what happens to people like her and you. Sensitive people. Intelligent people. People under pressure." He looked at her. "You don't have to think you're going mad. You're not."

247

The café door opened with a jangle of the bell and a gale of laughter from outside; two men in overalls came in, sharing a joke, greeting Stan noisily.

"I think I'll be all right," Kirsty said. "Now. I'm not going to drown myself, honestly."

"All the same. If it keeps happening, the panic attacks, you should see someone. A doctor. You shouldn't think you're all on your own."

"What about you?" Kirsty asked again. "Leaving home, leaving your parents?"

"I'm OK. I'm not letting them get to me, that's all. They killed Marianne, but they're not getting me."

"But the police? What if they find you, take you back?"

"They can try. They've already been to the shop, looking for me, but that was while I was still at Mrs Hendy's. Karim covered up, told them he hadn't seen me for weeks. They might come again, I suppose. But I'll be eighteen in three weeks, then I can do what I like. I might go home and tell them, my parents, what I'm doing and why, but I'm never going back. Not to stay."

"Mrs Hendy knew all the time where you were," Kirsty said. "She could have told them."

"Yes, I know."

"The old bitch, you called her once."

"I know. That wasn't fair – she's OK really. It was all that money that put me off at first."

Stan came down the aisle in his waddling, unhurried gait,

cleared cups on to a tray, glanced over at their table. "You two want anything else? Another coffee?"

"We're fine, thanks," Dally said. Kirsty had hardly touched her coffee. She drank some. Dally finished his and Stan took the cup away.

"You've left school as well?" Kirsty asked. "Were you meant to go to Oxford too?"

Dally shook his head. "I wouldn't make it. Even they had to admit that. But university, yes – an architect, that's what they wanted me to be, 'cos I was always good at art and design. As long as it was something that earned me lots of money, and something they could tell their friends. *Oh yes, our son's an architect. Doing frightfully well,*" Dally said in a posh voice. "That's what they want. *Our son's a dropout* doesn't give them quite the same kick."

"You weren't at my school, were you? Wolverton Park?"

"No." Dally smiled. "I'd have preferred that, but can you see my pushy parents sending me to the local comprehensive? I was at King Edward's. So was Karim, that's how I know him."

"The posh boys' school? The private one?"

"That's right. Why have me educated for nothing when they could fork out thousands a year to see me go off every morning in a smart black blazer? I dropped out of Year Twelve. I'm finished with school."

"What will you do now?"

"Stay on with Hassan for a while – Karim's brother. He lets me sleep on his floor. Work at the shop. Do more sculpting.

Maybe rent a room of my own, if I can find one cheap enough."

"You're not going away?"

"Away from where?"

"Away from here." Kirsty looked down. "Away from your parents. I mean, you easily could. There's nothing to keep you here any more, is there?"

"You," Dally said. "There's you."

She looked up, unable to read his expression. "Do you mean that?"

The answer she expected was: *I never say anything I don't mean. Don't you know that yet?* He didn't say it. He reached across the table to stroke her hand with the tip of his forefinger; as light as a moth's wing brushing along the back of her hand. He ran his fingertip down her index finger, until just the tips of their nails touched. Kirsty looked down at their hands, both of them roughened from work, with short chipped fingernails.

"There ought to be a spark," she said. "You know that famous painting?"

"Michelangelo, Sistine Chapel," Dally said. "I'm not a public schoolboy for nothing. There *is* a spark, can't you feel it?" He slid his hand away, then back so that his fingernail made contact with hers. He pretended an electric shock ran up his arm. "There it is again."

"You could go back to Mrs Hendy's," Kirsty said. "She was going to look for another gardener, but I bet she'd rather have you. She likes you. She thinks you're interesting, she told me."

"Yes, I might. After my birthday, when it doesn't make any difference whether the police know where I am or not. I liked it there. I like gardening."

"Then," Kirsty said, warming to the idea, "you could live in the cottage properly, with the water turned on and everything. You could have a *bathroom*, with hot water. And a *loo*. Think of the luxury."

Dally smiled. "Have you realized," he said, "now that I'm not squatting any more, as long as I keep out of view of the police, that we could meet each other now, like normal people do? If you want to, that is."

Kirsty looked at him. "There's no *if*," she said. "Don't you know that yet?"

CHAPTER 21

"Kirsty, darling." Ursula's voice crackled into Kirsty's ear, crisp and purposeful. "I know how upset you must be about Jay. I did *try* to prepare you, but – well. . ."

"I'm fine, thanks," Kirsty said, settling herself at the kitchen table to wait for the oven timer.

"But now you really *must* make an effort to get yourself organized for September. I've sent for some prospectuses for you and—"

"Mum. I'm not going anywhere. I'm staying here." Kirsty had forgotten to put plates out to warm. Cradling the phone between neck and shoulder, she reached carefully up to the high cupboard and brought two down to warm on the hob.

"Oh, but Kirsty – we've discussed this. I thought we agreed yes, with Jay there, it was going to be something like a business, but without him – well, it's nothing but menial work. Completely stultifying, I'd have thought, for someone of your intelligence. Now if I just tell you about this business studies course at—"

"Mum!" Kirsty shouted. "Will you *listen* to me?" There was an offended silence at the other end of the line. "I'm making plans of my own," she continued at normal volume.

"I'm staying here, and Lottie's coming in with me. We're going to build this up together. Jay's not the only person who can make it work."

"But you've got no business sense," her mother countered. "And neither, I imagine, has Lottie. Surely you have to admit that a little training would stand you in good stead, even if you do insist on toiling away as a stable girl? A diploma of some sort, HND?"

"Dad's going to take care of all that for us," Kirsty told her. "The accounts, the money."

"*Graham* is? Well, that just proves my point. He's got the financial sense of a flea. If you're going to rely on *him* to keep you solvent, you'll be bankrupt within a month. Do think about it carefully, Kirsty, that's all I ask. You'll be eighteen soon, without any qualifications whatsoever. A good business studies grounding would set you up for all kinds of opportunities –"

"Thanks, Mum, but I'm not doing it, OK? I'm staying here. You can't make me a clone of yourself! I'm doing it my own way!"

Again, the pointed silence; then, quietly, "All right, then, Kirsty. Since your mind's made up. When will I see you? I suppose you're too busy to come down to London."

Kirsty hesitated, thinking about testing herself, reaching the end of the tight-rope. The oven-timer buzzed; the kitchen was full of the warm smell of shepherd's pie.

"I could come for a day," she said. "I could do that."

*

"How's it going then, the writing?" she asked her father after their meal.

Graham was clearing the table. "OK, thanks. I've had a good day so far and I'll do a bit more tonight. Have you fed the cats, or shall I?"

Kirsty glanced down; Nutmeg was waiting by the empty bowl, giving plaintive glances at whoever came near. "I did feed them, earlier. I hope he doesn't need worming." She checked the calendar. "I'd better get some more pills." She found a Post-It note, wrote down *worm pills*, and stuck it to the fridge.

"You doing anything this evening?" Graham asked. "D'you want to look at the draft?"

"Dally's coming over," Kirsty said.

Graham's eyebrows rose. "Dally? The sexy gardener? The mysterious fugitive?"

"Yes. Actually he's not a gardener at the moment. He works in a record shop in town. That's who I went to see yesterday."

"They haven't caught up with him yet, then? The police?"

"No." Relenting, Kirsty sprinkled a few cat biscuits in Nutmeg's bowl. "He hasn't done anything, Dad. Only left home."

"Oh, is that all?" Graham poured water into the coffee machine. "So his parents are waiting desperately at home, are they?" He opened a paper filter and spooned coffee from the packet.

"He's eighteen next month, then he can do as he likes," Kirsty said. "Anyway, they deserve it. It's their fault."

Her father looked at her, then turned it into a joke. "It's a terribly difficult business, being a parent. There ought to be some qualification you have to get, before you're allowed to do it. We have to learn as we go along. And some of us are slow learners. But I am trying, Mouse."

He *was* trying. He had done the washing up, asked about the cats; he was making the coffee instead of waiting for Kirsty to bring it to him. She didn't expect him to change completely. She was wondering how and when she would introduce Dally to him. Tonight? No. Dally thought he was a shit. Perhaps Dally would change his mind, the way he had about Mrs Hendy.

"Dad – don't call me Mouse any more, OK?" Kirsty said.

Her father's eyebrows shot up, then lowered in a frown. "Don't you like it? Why on earth haven't you said so before?"

"I used not to mind. But I'd prefer to be Kirsty now. It was Jay's name for me, and Jay's gone now." Kirsty considered. "And I don't think I am a mouse, not really."

Graham looked at her, then gave a sudden laugh. "No, I suppose you're not. OK then, Mouse it isn't. You'll have to remind me, though." He looked at his watch. "What are you doing, when Dally comes round?"

"I don't know, really." Kirsty hadn't thought about it; it didn't seem to matter much. "Look at the horses. Walk. Talk. Nothing in particular."

"You will be careful, won't you," Graham said, giving her a significant look.

Kirsty flushed. "*Oh*, that's so typical of your generation! Instantly thinking about sex!" It was her own fault for having lied before, for pretending. "It's not the only thing there is, you know! And besides, I'm not a complete idiot—"

"You are, sometimes." He came over and gave her a hug. "Anyway, that's not the only thing I meant. I don't want you to get hurt, that's all." The kitchen filled with the rich smell of coffee; he fetched two mugs.

"I won't," Kirsty said, and found that she believed it. Other people might fail her, disappoint her – Jay, her father, her mother – but in Dally she had found the one person who would never let her down. But what if. . . ? she asked herself, uncertain of certainty; what if we get tired of each other, what if it doesn't work, what if he meets someone else?

No. There was no *if*.

In the quiet of the evening, Kirsty walked across the paddock to the far fence. She was leaving Leo out tonight, for the first time. He was grazing, moving steadily along the field-edge with his nose to the grass, taking no notice of her. Swifts screamed high overhead. Moths blundered in the warm air, blurring their wings.

With so many of her fears under control, Kirsty knew there was one that would never go away: the fear that someone would harm the horses. The two boys had been caught, but she had heard of other attacks, from time to time, elsewhere in the country. There was something about horses, their beauty and spirit, that provoked envy, the urge to stab and hurt. She would always be worrying, checking, coming out to the yard and fields at odd times, as long as she looked after horses.

Marianne must have come out alone, on a colder and less welcoming night than this, and stood looking at the river before taking her last steps, before letting the water take her. Kirsty felt Marianne's desperation in her own head; the urge to be rid of fears, anxieties, insecurities. And the voices: the voices that told her how easy it would be to walk into the dark water and let herself sink.

But Kirsty knew she wasn't going to follow. Her feet would take her down to the water's edge, but no further. The voices in her head were quiet now.

Yesterday, Dally had joked about a rehabilitation programme for her. "Cinema on a quiet Monday afternoon, three points. Underground train, ten points, extra for rush hour. Clubbing on a Saturday night, twenty. With a bonus if there's strobe lighting." She could make herself do it now, if she wanted to; but she didn't have to. For the moment there was nowhere she would rather be than here, in the spring dusk with its promise of summer, her yard jobs all finished and the stabled horses bedded down for the night. If she listened hard, she thought she could almost hear things growing; the rush of sap in the grass, the whisper of new leaves, the pulse of the earth itself.

She patted Leo's neck, smelled his warm horse smell, flicked a stray strand of mane over to the off-side of his neck; then saw that Dally was standing by the gate. He had come. Moth, a grey smoke cat coming from nowhere, stepped along the fence and paused with front feet up on the gate-post, arching his back to be stroked, butting his head into Dally's hand.

Kirsty waved. She walked across the paddock, leaving Leo to crop grass in the dusk and think whatever a horse thought.